MW01138565

KNIGHT'S FIRE

Scales of Honor Book One

SJ HIMES

CONTENTS

Foreword   v

Chapter 1   1
Chapter 2   4
Chapter 3   9
Chapter 4   18
Chapter 5   25
Chapter 6   36
Chapter 7   46
Chapter 8   54
Chapter 9   72
Chapter 10   80
Chapter 11   92
Chapter 12   106
Chapter 13   119
Chapter 14   127

Afterword   135
Also by SJ Himes   137
About the Author   139

COPYRIGHT

Knight's Fire © 2019 SJ Himes
Book One of Scales of Honor Series
All rights reserved.
Edited by Miranda Vescio.
Historical Accuracy Editing Services and Proofing provided by Royal Editing Services.
Cover by Sanja Gombar of Book Cover For You
https://bookcoverforyou.com/
No part of this book may be reproduced in any form or by any electronic or mechanical means including information storage and retrieval systems, without permission in writing from the author. The only exception is by a reviewer, who may quote short excerpts in a review.
This book is a work of fiction. Names, characters, places, and incidents either are products of the author's imagination or are used fictitiously. Any resemblance to actual persons, living or dead, events, or locales is entirely coincidental.
Digital piracy of ebooks kills indie authors. I can't write the books readers love if I can't make a living doing so. Please don't pirate my books. No one has permission to upload them or share them for any reason whatsoever. Don't download them for free.
This ebook edition is only for sale through Amazon and is enrolled in Kindle Unlimited. If you are reading it and did not legally purchase it or borrow it from Amazon, you have pirated this book. You have harmed my sales and are perpetuating harm against me and decreasing my ability to write the books I want and release them in a timely manner. Want more books from me? Don't pirate my books!
Please purchase your own copy and remember to review.

FOREWORD

Much of this world is based off of medieval Europe and medieval England, in terms of objects, tools, armor, clothing, etc. The Royal Sigil of Kentaine is borrowed from the flag of Wales. I include some words that are no longer in use today but are accurate for the time period in which this book is loosely set. Context has been provided around the words for better comprehension.

Thank you to Miranda for coming up with the book and series title. All of mine sucked.

And thank you to Alyson of Royal Editing Services--she helped me find my inner medieval fangirl.

DEDICATION

For every dragon who was denied a Happy Ever After.

"A dragon? That's unlikely." Gawain leaned back in the chair, stretching out his feet, wishing he could remove his heavy boots. A long day in the training yard with the new recruits left him exhausted, and he wasn't sure if the spring mud in the expansive yard or the absolute raw ineptitude of the recruits left him the weariest. A clump of mud fell off one of his boots and thumped to the floor in the queen's study. "Dragons haven't been seen in nearly a hundred years."

Queen Elise lifted a scroll, the red seal broken, and handed it to him. Her long blue dress whispered over the floor, the silks draping in a majestic manner. Everything his sister did was majestic—her crown might be heavy, but her spine was made of iron. She daintily sidestepped the mud and paced while Gawain unrolled the parchment scroll and read the missive from one of his knights, a trustworthy man who was assigned to the northern border villages a few years before. Evern was an experienced warrior and not prone to fits of whimsy.

"A dragon sighted in the hills outside of Morvain," Gawain

murmured. "Livestock is missing, and a hunting party sent after it came back heavily injured and reporting nightmarish tales of a great beast with a scaly hide and breathing fire." Gawain looked back to his sister, and he lifted a brow. "No one died?"

"Three hunters were burned, and the injuries are severe." Elise sighed. Worry creased her otherwise smooth brow, and her dark green eyes were clouded, fears he understood better than most buried in their depths. His elder by a handful of years, she had always confided in him, even when they were children. "Along with mismatched descriptions of the beast in question, their stories are inconsistent. The only things that are certain are the missing livestock and the injuries to the hunters. I am sending a healer and a contingent of soldiers to Morvain, and I want you to lead the mission."

Gawain quirked a brow at his sister, but as the older sibling, she was impervious to his typically formidable stare. "I'll go, but I wonder why you're sending me."

"If it is a dragon, I'd like to avoid a mass panic and mobs of frightened villagers killing anything in their path into the hills. By sending my brother along with some of our best soldiers, I am trying to stamp out any mob mentality disasters."

Gawain smirked and carefully rose to his feet, handing the scroll back to his sister. "I'd rather take a mage along instead of just a healer. Tristan is a powerful one and a capable healer who can manage traumatic injuries as well. We may need the support if we come face to face with a being that can wield magic. What do you want me to do about the dragon?"

"I trust your judgment. See if you can't figure out what's going on. If dragons are returning to our lands, I want to avoid conflict." Elise gestured to her desk, the wide surface littered with scrolls and leather-bound books. A large, heavy ring with a deep blood-red ruby glittered from her left ring finger, the crest of their family emblazoned within the wide band of silver. "Our chronicles tell of intelligent beings with the ability to speak and powerful magics. I don't want to start a war with the dragons if they are returning to our lands, and I don't want our people killing intelligent beings as if they are animals."

"Then I need to leave as soon as possible, preferably before this evening." Gawain leaned down and pressed a kiss to his sister's cheek. She took it with a soft smile and a brief hug. "I best get started."

"Be careful, little brother," Elise called after him as he strode for the far door leading from the queen's chambers. "Bring me back a dragon!" Her words were teasing, but he would if it was at all possible. A dragon in Kentaine, something that hadn't happened in over a hundred years, would be a spectacle indeed. The large wooden doors carved with the royal crest of Kentaine were opened by two royal guards in their red and black armor, velvet tabards bearing a red dragon in flight on a black field rustling when they bowed briefly as he passed.

Morvain, a small village at the foot of the mountain range that made up the kingdom of Kentaine's northern and eastern borders, was a three-day ride to the northeast. His boots rang on the polished stone floors, thoughts full of what and who he would need to bring on the mission. He'd need supplies for the journey, as a full squadron of men and their horses would consume more than the small villages would be able to provide. Tents, wagons, and mounted knights. He thought about infantry, but the delay in getting them to Morvain in any acceptable timeframe wasn't an option. Three days to the village mounted, over a week by foot.

2

Gawain resisted the urge to doze in the saddle, keeping alert despite the warmth of the spring sun and the cooling breeze flowing down from the hills. The days had been gentle, the sight of the forests and fields coming alive with new growth and bright green leaves enough to soothe the small thread of nerves that ran through his thoughts. They were making good time, and the knights and their combined retinue would reach Morvain in a matter of hours, probably just before sunset. He'd sent the scout, Sora, ahead to alert the village of their arrival.

The retinue would camp outside the village at a suitable location since Morvain was too small to have an inn or stables large enough to hold their animals. A scout, six knights, a mage and his mount, their own individual retinues, and the portable smithy slowed the procession, but the royal roads out to Morvain were tended every spring and in decent shape, and their animals were fresh. Fair weather sped them along, and they would arrive able to do their duty with minimal downtime.

The sun warmed his armor, and he was thankful he wasn't

wearing the full complement of gear. He wore a leather gambeson, padded linen and silk-lined leather trousers with knee-high leather boots spelled to stay dry and avoid blisters, and a black surcoat with a red dragon flying on a black field. The heavier pieces of his armor were in the wagons. The rest of his knights were outfitted in a like manner. Conflict on the road in this part of the country was unlikely, and they needed to spare their horses the weight since they would be in the saddle for most of the day. He wore his half-shield strapped to his back by its guige, keeping the cool wind off his shoulders, and his sword and dirk rested in the scabbards on his hips, adjusted to keep the ends from smacking his horse in the sides.

A screech from high above had Gawain squinting against the setting sun. A gyrfalcon swooped down out of the light and landed on the gloved hand of the mage riding beside him. Skilled in combat magic and battlefield medicine, Tristan de Lyons was a formidable, dangerous man and one of his oldest friends. They were distant cousins as well, their grandparents were siblings, though Gawain and Tristan looked nothing alike. Tristan favored Elise more than Gawain did, Gawain inheriting black hair and blue eyes from his mother and Tristan and Elise favoring the blonder, more golden tones in hair and skin of the rest of their family. The three of them spent their childhoods causing mischief in the castle and the surrounding countryside, at least until Elise's courses in governing became more arduous and Gawain and Tristan went into different vocations. Gawain followed the sword, and Tristan his magic.

Tristan pet his gyrfalcon with a finger, smoothing down its ruffled feathers. His midnight blue robes fluttered in the wind, his blond hair lifting from his brow as he settled the raptor, calming it with a few whispered words and a soft touch.

"Any news?" Gawain asked, straightening in the saddle. The surrounding hillsides were a mix of thickened stands of trees and brush and rolling fields of lush grass and early flowers. In the far distance, the peaks of mountains were still laden with snow and ice, but in the lower reaches of the range, life was returning. That meant prey animals were increasing in number, and predators along with them. The road was in frequent use from travelers, merchants, and the military, so larger predators kept to the wilder reaches of the looming forest, but there were still some of the more dangerous solitary predators about that could be worrisome, even to mounted knights.

Tristan hummed, making eye contact and holding it with the bird for a long moment before he blinked and rested his hand on the pommel of his saddle, the raptor preening its feathers, job completed. Tristan dug out a couple slices of rabbit meat from a small satchel attached to his saddle, feeding the bird as he gathered his thoughts. "Merlin saw some signs of fire in the higher ranges: blackened trees, burnt fields. Nothing widespread though, just a few isolated spots coming in from over the pass and closer to Morvain. Looks like a trail. A few days old, maybe closer to over a week at the oldest locations."

"Dragons?"

Tristan nodded. "It aligns with a feeding dragon. The chronicles speak of dragons preferring to burn their kills, eating them charred."

"Can you sense any magic?"

Tristan grimaced and shook his head once. "Too far away yet. I'll be able to tell you for certain once we get to the village."

"Keep an eye out," Gawain cautioned, and Tristan clucked to his bird before lightly tossing the raptor into the air. Merlin gave a cheerful sounding call and swooped away, gaining height and quickly disappearing. Tristan could see through Merlin's eyes, their connection granting him access to the raptor's senses.

Gawain looked back over his shoulder and got a nod from Avril and Bedivere, who rode directly behind him and Tristan. Felix and Silfur rode behind them, and Axton brought up the rear, the young man newly knighted by Elise the month before. Three squires drove the wagons behind the knights, hand-picked from the newest batch of recruits. Two lasses and a lad, the three of them the most level-headed and the least likely to panic. Avril was his most seasoned knight of the six, and she had the squires well in hand for this excursion.

The wind picked up, fluffy white clouds racing across the sky from over the mountains. The banner bearing the Red Dragon emblem of the royal family snapped and tugged in the uptick. With the wind came the sound of hooves on the packed gravel road, and Gawain lifted a hand to shield his eyes from the sun, seeing a rider round the bend of the road where it curved up into the hills. Tension lifted from his shoulders when he recognized his scout, the young woman's red hair streaming out behind her.

He relaxed until she drew closer, her roan gelding's sides heaving as she drew him to a halt and whirled him around to keep pace with his warhorse. Sora was pale and sweaty, and road dust layered her skin and clothing.

"My prince, the village," she gasped out. Tristan tossed him a flagon of water, kept cold by spells, and he handed it over to Sora, who took it gratefully. She drank quickly, stoppered the flagon, then gestured back up the road. "There's been a sighting of the beast. The villagers are talking about going out in numbers and killing it."

"Has it harmed anyone?" Gawain asked, even as he lifted his right arm and made a fist, drawing them to a halt.

"A farmer's pig went missing in the night, but no people

7

have been harmed since the hunters a few days back. I saw no proof it was a dragon, but the villagers are riled up. A farmer's lad claims he saw the dragon on the edge of a pasture this morning. The farmer is calling for a mob to hunt it down. It's going to be a disaster if they find the dragon."

Gawain spun his warhorse around, the stallion snorting, rousing from its lassitude brought on by the warm and sunny day. His knights waited for orders. "Axton, stay with the retinue, make your way to the village and set up camp. I want things in order before last bell." The young knight nodded, no reluctance showing at missing any action. "The rest of us are heading there now. Sora, swap out your horse; we leave once you're ready."

A squire jumped down from the lead wagon and ran back along the string to fetch Sora's spare mount. She dismounted and broke down her saddle, tossing it up onto a bay gelding with long legs and a build meant for speed that Mel, the squire, brought up from the rear. Mere minutes later, Gawain whirled his warhorse around and, with Sora leading the way, took off for the village.

3

Wing drooping, Zephyr whimpered and moved carefully through the underbrush, wishing he could fly. The deep gash on the first wing joint wept blood, and he licked at the wound, hoping it wouldn't tear more and leave a trail behind him. The injuries on his wrists and ankles stung, but they weren't as deep as the cut on his wing. A small bush scraped over the cut as he went deeper into the woods, and he hissed through his fangs, smoke escaping in small puffs. He swallowed back the fire building in his throat, not wanting to give the humans he could hear in the far distance anything to track. His magics were still depleted, exhausted from his escape and the flight over the mountains, and he only had enough energy to disguise his tracks as he crawled through the damp undergrowth.

Belly aching, Zephyr sniffed as he sought a cave or overhang that he could squeeze into and hide. He couldn't manage a full transformation, but if he found a place close enough to his current size, he might be able to make himself fit. Depleted as he was, changing his size by a few degrees was manageable, but he fervently wished that he could pull off a whole transformation. Taking the form of another creature would enable him to hide better than hoping for a cave he could fit within. He needed to conserve his energy, and growing smaller might not be the best idea if he was cornered, but he was running out of options. At least he still had his fire.

The rocky cliff face rose out of the trees and most of the brush fell away. He was losing cover, but his nose picked up the scent of fresh water and moss, and there was a chill emanating from where the rocks piled up at the base of the cliff. He crouched behind a large boulder, twisting his long neck, and his sharp eyes picked up a deep recess in the earth where the ground smoothed out. A faint hint of bear and other smaller critters came from within, but there were no signs of anything living in the cave aside from the tiny hints of mice. They were too small to be worth the trouble to dig out, so Zephyr ignored them and pulled back, looking behind him and down the hillside.

There was a bit of a plateau at the base of the cliff before the cleared area sloped down into the woods. Brush and some stunted trees grew among the boulders and broke up the shadows. The sun was setting behind the cliff, and the shadows were deeper where he stood than they were a few yards to the side where the sun still cast down its light. Light glinted off the pond on the outskirts of the village, and he could see the farms and pastures through the trees.

He had tried to approach the humans, hoping for someone to help him, but they had reacted in fear. The hungry bear stealing pigs from the farms along the edge of the village wasn't helping. Hunger overrode its instinct to avoid humans, and the livestock was too appealing. Humans had come after him with spears and ropes, and his control was negligible after his long ordeal. When he had been awakened from a fitful doze with a sharp spear in his face, he'd reacted badly. Thankfully, he hadn't killed anyone, but after expending what little energy he had left to stave off the worst of the burns the humans received, the sound of more humans approaching forced him to run. The villagers wouldn't look kindly on him after nearly killing some of them, even if it was in self-defense.

Hoping the humans would still think he was in the woods, Zephyr crawled into the cave, ducking low. He pulled in his injured wing as close to his side as he could, the joint screaming at him, and wiggled until he could turn around, tail curled around his rear quarters and his wings furled in. He shuffled to the side a bit more and relaxed the injured wing as much as he could, letting it extend and take pressure off the wound. He sighed, a bit of smoke drifting toward the top of the cave. It was a snug fit, but he could lift his head a fair bit and see past the boulders to the clearing outside the cave. Thankful it was big enough and he didn't need to expend magic to make his mass smaller, Zephyr did his best to relax and rest.

Hunger ate at his stomach, and he sighed, knowing he would need to leave the safety of the cave once it grew dark to hunt for food. Maybe the bear would return to the cave and he'd get to fill his belly and take care of the villagers' problem with the same kill.

Thinking of meat made his hunger increase, and he lowered his head to the smooth earth of the cave floor. Zephyr stared out through the spaces between the boulders, watching the sky in the far distance and wishing he was among the clouds racing across the blue horizon.

He smelled the humans before he heard them. Opening his eyes a mere slit, since they would reflect the light back from any torches carried by the humans, Zephyr waited. The cave was quiet, but the stone walls and the cliff outside made the humans' calls to each other bounce about the valley, increasing in volume as they drew nearer to his hiding place. Twilight came while he dozed, purple and dark blue hues seeping across the tiny bit of sky he could see.

Zephyr curled up as tightly as he could and tucked his head under his injured wing, hiding his eyes. It didn't sound like they'd found the cave yet, but they might soon. He cursed himself for his foolishness—the villagers might know about the cave and check it.

His magic was nothing but a wisp of smoke in the center of his being—years of being drained of his magics and too few years of developing his abilities before his capture meant his magic was as stunted as his natural physical form, which was smaller than it should be for his age. Managing a transformation into an innocuous creature like a cave bat or even disguising himself as part of the rock walls was beyond him. Hopeless and despairing of his weakness, he shivered in tense anticipation.

Voices grew closer, and Zephyr was faced with an impossible choice—let them kill him or kill humans in self-defense. He didn't want to die so soon after gaining his freedom.

Gawain drew his horse to a stop next to Sora's gelding, the scout slipping from the saddle and kneeling in the damp grass of the pasture that abutted the tree line on the outside of the village. They were in the narrow space between the fence and the woods, and Avril and Tristan held mage lights aloft, the soft white light gently illuminating the deepening shadows as the sun dipped toward the horizon. Sunset was in mere minutes, and they had just arrived in the village, riding on Sora's heels as they cut through the small village center and heading for the spot where the pig went missing that morning. The village had been all but deserted as they rode through, small children and older women milling near the square, and small pinpricks of torchlight glinting in the distance amongst the trees, telling them that the mob was out in full force. They had no time left.

"Bear," Sora declared confidently, getting back to her feet and brushing damp earth from her knees. "Paw prints are distinctive. It went through the fence rails, took the pig, and dragged it back out the same way it went in." She grabbed the saddle and swung back up, collecting the reins as her eyes traced the marks in the earth toward the woods. "I bet a month's worth of stipends that we'll find the remains a few yards within the tree line."

"How did the villagers not notice it was a bear?" Tristan wondered, disbelief in his tone. "I think they'd know what bear tracks look like?"

"Why bother looking for clues when there's a dragon to worry about?" Avril responded, and she looked out over the forest. "Most of the torches I can see are heading up the ridgeline towards the cliffs. If you were a dragon and needed to hide, where would you go?"

"A cave," Tristan answered, and Gawain swore under his breath. They were running out of time.

"We need to hurry." Gawain gestured to Tristan, who nodded curtly before closing his eyes and lifting his arms out to his side.

The mage muttered softly until his torso glowed with a blinding light, miniature suns, the size of apples, erupting from him. The tiny balls of white light shot out and up by the hundreds, a wave of soundless flame dancing in the wind before shooting out in front of them in a widening arc through the trees. Shouted curses and startled exclamations came from those hunting in the trees as they returned the forest to daytime brightness. The light flickered among the trees like fire, but the orbs were not made of flame, so the forest was in no danger of becoming an inferno.

Tristan dropped his arms and swayed for a second, grabbing the wide, wooden pommel and leaning over it as he breathed heavily for a moment. "I can hold the constellation spell for a short while."

"Forget the bear," Gawain said to his knights. "Stop the villagers from getting to the dragon."

"If the dragon attacks us?" Bedivere asked, face grim.

"Hope we have time to talk it out of killing us all," Gawain replied. "Let's go."

He guided them into the forest. The tiny suns lit the way, allowing his horse to find his footing and letting them race ahead without fear of their mounts tripping or branches knocking them from their saddles.

Smoke from torches wafted into the cave. His pursuers were close. Too close. Zephyr could retreat no farther, and he shook, despairing. He didn't want to hurt anyone, but with his magic depleted, all he had were his fangs, claws, and fire. Humans were easily broken and burnt, and he refused to kill anyone. His end was approaching, beaten with farming tools and stabbed by spears. Unless he ran away, but he was weakened by hunger and his injuries weren't healing, so he would run until he could run no more then die where he fell. Dying alone was a horrible way to perish, but it was better than being trapped in a cave and stabbed to death or dragged back into hell and chained for eternity to a madman.

He hoped it wouldn't hurt too badly. As he peered around the edge of his wing, he could see torchlight glowing at the entrance of the cave and shadows of people dancing across the stone. He would make a run for it the first chance he got.

A torch was thrust into the cave, and an angry face came into view long enough to see him in the shadows. "The beast! It's in the cave!"

Zephyr growled, sharp and menacing, and the human ducked out of sight with a yelp. Shouts echoed from outside and more humans gathered. It was too narrow for them to charge inside and the floor sloped. He hoped they didn't have bows or crossbows. His scales would deflect most arrows, but the thin membranes of his wings were vulnerable at this range, and enough rips and tears in them could lead to massive blood loss.

A spear came thrusting in from outside, and Zephyr dodged it, snapping his jaws just behind the sharp head, the wood splintering in his teeth. The haft was yanked back, and Zephyr spit out the spear head, the metal landing with a *thunk*. A disgruntled human grumbled, and another moved into the cave entrance, peering inside. Zephyr growled, but this man, a broad-shouldered human who smelled of hot metal and fire, just grinned back at him.

"Fierce beast," the man said, menace in his tone. "Your skull will look great over my forge. I'm going to bash your brains in." The muscles in his arms and the scents coming off the thick leathers he wore told Zephyr this man was a blacksmith, and the human reached back for something. A large hammer was handed over and Zephyr snarled, tensing.

The human crouched, almost too big to enter the cave, and he lowered the hand holding the hammer enough that he couldn't swing. Zephyr lashed out with his tail and smacked the human in the chest. He pulled his tail back to avoid a wild swing of the hammer, and the human was knocked back on his ass, coughing, a hand to his chest. The hammer fell, the human retching as he struggled for air.

Some other humans grabbed the smith and dragged him away from the cave, and Zephyr saw a few people with bows in hand. He was in trouble. He roared, the sound reverberating out of the cave, and the humans cringed back, a couple dropping their bows and running. Zephyr dragged in a deep breath and let out a torrent of flame, sending more people running and shouting. No one was injured from what he could see, and if he kept flaming as they approached, he could keep them at bay for a bit. Not indefinitely, but it bought him some time.

Gawain led the charge up the hill, Tristan sending out a wave of the bright white orbs ahead of them. Villagers were clustered a few yards away from the cave that was illuminated by the torchlight and the miniature suns, and the air was thick with the smell of smoke.

"Hold!" Gawain shouted, and the villagers turned toward them as Gawain guided his mount into the crowd, forcing people back away from the cliff face, his knights doing the same behind him.

"I am Sir Gawain, First Knight of Kentaine, Justiciar of the High Courts, brother of Queen Elise, and I order you all to stand down!" Gawain's shout brought the milling crowd to a shocked halt, and at his sides, Avril and Bedivere drew their swords, pushing their mounts forward, causing the villagers to stumble back. Many of them carried weapons—some spears, farming implements, and one burly man dressed in smithy gear carried a large hammer. Silfur and Felix drew to a halt on either side of Avril and Bedivere, with Tristan behind them all. The mage dismounted and headed for the cave, the mounted knights making a wall between the villagers and the cave.

The smith and a tall, thin man pushed through the crowd to stop next to Gawain's mount, both eyeing the warhorse, who snorted and stamped his great hooves, warily. "Your Highness, I am Ethan, an elder of the village of Morvain. The dragon is inside the cave. You've arrived in time to help us kill it."

"Elder Ethan, there will be no killing this night," Gawain retorted, and the villagers murmured unhappily among themselves. "Stand down. Where is Sir Evern?" Gawain took a quick glance over his shoulder, seeing Tristan kneeling just outside the cave, peering inside. He heard a soft whisper and figured Tristan was talking to the dragon. Talking was better than a conflagration anytime. He needed to disperse the villagers and give Tristan time.

The elder frowned at Gawain, obviously unhappy. "Your knight is in the woods, tracking a bear. Bears don't shoot fire from their jaws and burn people. He's wasting his time."

Evern likely knew it was a bear attacking the livestock and probably went after it to show the townsfolk the real culprit. One knight against dozens of villagers wasn't good odds, so Gawain couldn't fault the man. "Silfur, Felix, go find Sir Evern and the bear. Take care of that problem then check in with Axton and the retinue. Return here once you've gotten things sorted out."

"Yes, sir," Silfur said, and with a nod, she and Felix turned their mounts and headed back for the woods. Avril and Bedivere remained in place, formidable and intimidating. Many of the villagers were quiet, eyeing the mounted knights with trepidation, weapons and tools lowered. "Avril, Bedivere, mind the crowd. I'll see to Tristan."

Gawain dismounted, and the villagers backed away even more. The smith glared at him, hammer braced on his shoulder, the big man bulging with muscles. Gawain wasn't as bulky or as tall, but he wasn't worried about the smith. He wouldn't discount him as a threat, but he was confident enough he could handle the man if he tried to cause trouble. Gawain met the elder's unhappy gaze. "Disperse your people. Head back to the village."

The elder opened his mouth to argue, but Gawain held up a gloved hand and shook his head. "I will speak to you later. Take your people home. Goodnight, Elder."

Elder Ethan grimaced, but he gave a curt nod. "Very well, Your Highness."

"Just Sir Gawain is fine." He was technically a prince and his sister's heir as long as she remained unwed and without issue, but he hadn't gone by His Highness since he was knighted. Queen Elise wasn't fond of him setting aside his royal titles, so her compromise was to name him First Knight of the Realm, a title that hadn't existed in the past, and give him the authority to claim his own personal squadron of knights as vassals. In the capital, at court, and in the castle, he was still His Royal Highness, but amongst his knights and close friends, he chose to be known as Sir Gawain. He preferred the knighthood over being a prince anyway. Gawain handed the reins to Bedivere with a nod and walked to the cave, leaving the elder to send his people home.

Tristan still knelt at the cave entrance, and he met Gawain's gaze with a frustrated twist of his lips. "We might have a problem," Tristan said quietly when Gawain crouched beside him.

"Is it not a dragon?" Maybe the villagers had cornered the bear and thought it was the dragon? How deep was the cave?

"It's a dragon all right," Tristan whispered back, frowning.

"What's wrong then? Can it not talk?" Many of the legends said the dragons could speak just like people.

"He can talk," Tristan complained. "He just won't talk to me."

Gawain was about to speak, when a distinctly inhuman and melodic voice came out from the shadows in the cave. "I will not talk to the mage, but I will speak to the knight."

The mage terrified him. This one smelled of magic and royal blood and had the power to enslave him, and Zephyr wanted nothing to do with the man. He snarled and wished he'd never tried to seek help from humans in the first place. They were too easily scared and attacked when frightened. Mages were dangerous and hurt more of Zephyr's kind than any other people. The madman he escaped from was a mage of royal blood, and he didn't trust the blond mage who tried to speak with him.

When the knight came, Zephyr blinked in surprise. He smelled of royal blood, and there was the faintest hint of magic clinging to him. Not surprising, since many royal families had some magic in their blood, but this man had almost none. Maybe enough to light a candle, almost nothing compared to the man beside him. The mage glowed with power, and their scents were alike enough that the knight and mage must be related. The knight was lean and moved like a predator but without the malice that clung to most dangerous men. Zephyr took a slow, deep breath, and parsed the scents even further, finding nothing but sweat from a long day in the saddle and a slight edge of adrenaline.

They must have rushed to get to him, though Zephyr had no idea why. The knight had a close-cropped black beard, long black hair tied back at the nape of his neck, and blue eyes that matched the evening sky. Skin tanned gold from days in the sun, and a strong heartbeat Zephyr could hear despite the angry mob outside the cave. The other knights' voices filtered into the cave, directing the people to return to their homes, and they were obeying, albeit reluctantly.

He wouldn't be killed by a mob this night.

Zephyr had surprised himself by speaking. He rarely did because he was afraid of human reactions. Humans had a hard time dealing with a creature speaking words they could understand while looking like an animal. Humans were weird.

The knight knelt, a hand on the pommel of his sword. Not to draw it, but to hold the sword out of the way so he could get low enough to get a better look into the cave. A tiny star of white fire swooped into the cave, but it was cold and didn't hurt. The shadows fell back, and the knight blinked in surprise when he saw Zephyr curled inside the cave.

A soft smile lit his face, and Zephyr ducked behind his wing, peeking around the edge with one eye. The knight gazed at him with a gentle expression, and Zephyr was struck by a sudden shyness.

"Hello, dragon." The knight took a long look at Zephyr, from tail tip to head, and Zephyr marveled when the knight lingered on the injuries on his legs and wing. "I am Sir Gawain, First Knight of Kentaine. I mean you no harm."

"The mage," Zephyr whispered. "He scares me."

Gawain glanced at the mage, who was surprised. Gawain spoke to Zephyr gently. "The mage is my cousin, Tristan. He is a good man who would like to help you. We grew up together, and I trust him with my life and the lives of my knights. I promise he will not hurt you."

"No mage," Zephyr whispered and hid behind his wing. Or he tried—the tiny star made it hard for him to hide.

The knight spoke softly to the mage, who agreed to give them space. He waited while the mage got to his feet and left, though the tiny star remained.

"May I sit?"

Zephyr peeked, and the knight was watching him carefully. He gave a small dip of his muzzle, and the knight maneuvered himself to sit on his rear, stretching out his legs with a low groan. "I apologize. We've been riding for the last few days to get here, and my legs are sore." He paused and gestured at Zephyr. "You're hurt."

"I escaped," Zephyr said quietly, finding it hard to look away from the knight. He was pretty, in a way he rarely found humans to be. Maybe it was his voice. Gawain looked scary but sounded kind. He never knew a man such as this to be kind.

"It takes courage to escape," Gawain replied. "Do you need help? It's what I'm here for."

Zephyr squinted at the knight. "You came to help me?"

Gawain smiled and made a vague gesture with his hand. "I came to contact the dragon sighted in these hills and stop violence. Helping you is part of that." Gawain gave him a small smile. "But I would help you regardless. You seem to need it."

Zephyr hummed, thinking. Gawain made no aggressive moves, his blue eyes were very pretty, and he didn't smell angry or mean. Zephyr wished again for his magic to return so he could see the human's aura, but all he got was a vague impression of sincerity and a kind heart.

"You would help me? I burned the humans who tried to hurt me."

Gawain grimaced. "I won't lie—that may be a problem, but Tristan can help the humans you burned. Did you mean to kill them?"

"No!" Zephyr said sharply then ducked behind his wing, cringing instinctively. If he'd spoken to his captor like that, Zephyr would've been beaten. There was no sound from Gawain, and after a long moment, Zephyr calmed himself then peeked again. Gawain gazed at him with a heartbroken expression, eyes dark, then he gave Zephyr a short nod. "All right, dragon. Self-defense is all I need to know. I'll handle the villagers."

"Zephyr."

"Pardon?"

"My name is Zephyr."

5

Never in his entire life did Gawain ever think he would meet a dragon face to face, much less speak to one. To be talking to a dragon now was amazing, but Gawain's heart broke with every exchange with him.

Zephyr was small, and Gawain could count his ribs beneath his scales. Scars littered his sides and the parts of his hindquarters Gawain could see with the small dragon curled up inside the cave. He was about the height of a large warhorse, but slimmer, and his body was much longer and very flexible. It struck him in a moment of dissonance that calling a being the size of a warhorse small wasn't logical, but in his mind, dragons were larger than houses and capable of toppling towers.

Long wings folded up, the dragon curled in like a cat in a basket. He had four legs, two wings, and a very long tail—a dragon from ancient lore and not the more common wyrm sighted in the distant mountains. His neck was long, about a third of the tail's length, but it doubtless gave him the ability to turn and see and strike with dexterity.

His scales were dulled by lack of care and malnutrition but were a pretty combination of red and fiery oranges and black, much like a fox in its autumn colors. Short spikes with dulled tips lined parts of his neck and his head, and Gawain kept the flinch off his face when he catalogued the deliberate clipping of claws and the trimmed spikes along the tail. A long muzzle with sharp teeth and a wide skull with large eyes peered back at him, and when Zephyr came out from hiding behind his wing, Gawain saw the faded scales around his neck, as if rubbed down by friction from a collar.

Zephyr had been collared like an animal and mistreated horribly. Anger welled up in his belly, but he kept it off his face. Zephyr behaved as if he expected to be hit at any minute, terribly hand shy and scared.

"A beautiful name," Gawain murmured, and Zephyr tilted his head to the side, blinking at him from one large eye. It was a strange shade of orange, not glaring, but subtle, softer, like embers burning low in ashes. The iris was slitted like a cat, and he smiled when an inner eyelid swept across the large eye from the corner before the ridge above the eye twitched and Zephyr blinked the outer lid.

They stared at each other for a long while, and Gawain found himself relaxing, even with the cold night air creeping through his armor and his knights watching carefully from a short distance away. Zephyr lowered his head to the dirt, staring up at Gawain, and the small dragon reminded him so much of a cat he was expecting to hear a soft purr come out from the long neck. Gawain yawned and shook his head.

"We shouldn't sleep here," Gawain said, and Zephyr blinked up at him, but didn't move. The dragon was weak, and Gawain hoped he could walk. Staying in the cave wasn't an option—they needed to move Zephyr to their camp so Tristan could treat his injuries. "Can you walk?"

"Tired," came a sleepy whisper, and Zephyr tucked his

head under his wing, his whole body shuddering with a deep sigh.

"Don't fall asleep just yet," Gawain cautioned, though he knew it was a losing battle. The poor thing was exhausted.

Gawain got to his feet carefully, a bit stiff from sitting on the damp ground, and walked to his knights.

Avril and Bedivere had dismounted, and the villagers were gone. Sora was still mounted, facing in the direction of the woods, keeping watch. Tristan came to his side once he left the cave entrance.

His knights faced him expectantly, and Tristan was all but vibrating with curiosity. He gave them a reassuring nod. "The dragon's name is Zephyr. Young, from what I can guess, and he bears signs of abuse and captivity."

Avril gasped, and Bedivere's hand fell to his sword. Gawain spoke to his cousin. "I need you to head to the village and take care of the people who were burned. Zephyr burned them in self-defense."

"The dragon needs healing too," Tristan said, and Gawain nodded in agreement.

"He does, but he needs food and sleep first. Heal the humans—they were burned by dragon fire, and we need tensions eased with the village. Any word from the others?"

They all heard the hoofbeats at the same time and turned toward the sound. Felix broke out of the tree line and lifted an arm, hand open. Gawain sighed in relief. "Camp has been established. Good. We need to go."

"Can the dragon be moved?" Bedivere asked, but Tristan spoke up even as he headed for his mount.

"If he can walk, get him out of the cave and to camp. I can't treat him effectively in the cave, and I don't want us trapped up here with our backs to the cliff if the villagers object to the dragon staying here." Tristan mounted, and Avril went for her horse, swinging up quickly, all but reading

Gawain's mind. Tristan was a capable fighter, but he could be vulnerable to attack when focusing on his spellwork.

Tristan spurred his mount to a trot, and Avril followed. Felix rode up at a jog. "How far is camp?" Gawain called.

"Half a league down the hillside toward the road. There's an old orchard with a narrow access road. The retinue has the tents set up, and supper is cooking. Evern is still tracking the bear, and Axton went after him with some crossbows once camp was established." Axton and Evern were both capable hunters, and the cavalry crossbows shot heavy, armor piercing bolts that should solve the bear problem in short order.

"Closer than I was expecting. We should be able to get there quickly," Gawain headed back for the cave. "Let me get our new friend."

Zephyr stumbled, and the gentle knight swung down from his huge horse. "We're almost there, I promise." A hand hovered over his head but didn't touch. Zephyr smelled leather and horse and man and got to his feet. There was naught but soft grass under his paws and the trees were tall. Campfires burned not far off, and Zephyr grumbled but began to walk toward the camp.

The knight, Gawain, did not remount and stayed at his side, casting concerned glances at him with each whimper and halting step Zephyr took. "I am sorry. I didn't know you were this weak. We should have stayed at the cave."

Zephyr didn't reply, too tired to speak. The warhorse plodded along, and Zephyr was pleased it didn't shy away from him. The other warhorses the knights rode were just as calm, though the knights themselves eyed him warily. The mage wasn't present, and that was the only reason Zephyr followed Gawain out of the cave and into the forest.

At some point, they reached the camp, firelight and the sound of humans talking quietly blurred together. Scents and sensations jumbled together, and Zephyr stumbled again, but this time, he landed on something soft and sweet smelling. He blinked, and Gawain was there, voice distant.

"Zephyr? Can you hear me?"

"Hmm?"

"Can I help? May I touch you?"

He was too weak to object, yet Gawain waited for permission to touch him. He gave a tiny nod, and warm hands went to his wings and helped arrange them on the soft things beneath him. Zephyr sighed, enjoying Gawain's hands running over his scales, and fell asleep instantly, feeling safe for the first time in a very long time.

The wonderful scent of roasted beef woke him, and

Zephyr dived on the chunk of steaming meat before he was even fully awake. It was delicious, the best thing he'd tasted in longer than he could remember, and it was gone in seconds.

A chuckle made him look up, and Gawain smiled down at him. They were in a large tent, and Zephyr realized the soft things he'd laid upon were large pillows covered in something very smooth and soft. He sniffed and smelled feathers, linen, and silkworms. The shelter was vaguely rectangular with a slanted roof that came to a pinnacle in two places, the tops of the tent held aloft by a shimmering spell and a wooden framework. The hum of magic was subtle, and the walls of the tent were thin enough to let some light in, but not the wind. Sunlight illuminated tent decorations, some inside and out. There was a large emblem stitched on the front of the tent, but his eyes and mind couldn't make sense of what it could be, aside from the colors of red and black. Some kind of animal perhaps. The rest of the tent was a light linen color that glowed under the morning sun.

"Hungry, I see," Gawain said, and the knight moved aside a portion of the tent with one arm. Bright sunlight landed inside, a hint of dew and warming grasses carried on the soft breeze. Gawain's arms were bare up to his shoulders, skin a soft golden color and muscles rippling as he moved.

It was morning. He barely remembered getting to the camp and had slept through the night. Gawain looked down at him with some concern. "Let me get you more food. Stay here, all right?"

Zephyr dropped his head to the pillows, and Gawain ducked out of the tent. The ceiling was high above, plenty of room to stand if he wanted, and it was big enough he was able to stretch out. His wings would hit the sides if he opened them fully, but they were comfortable in the space he had, and his tail might slip out under the far edge of the fabric, but not by much. Zephyr shuffled around a bit and managed an easy curl on the pillows, closing his eyes and sinking into the warmth they offered.

"I have more beef." Gawain entered the tent carrying a large platter, biceps bulging a bit from the weight of the meat. "We bought a cow off one of the farmers. We eat our food cooked, but if you prefer, I can get a raw shank in here instead."

"Fire cooked is good," Zephyr whispered, his words hissing a bit. The evil mage who held him captive fed him raw meat, and while that was adequate, dragons preferred to char their kills for easier digestion.

He wasn't used to humans waiting on him. Gawain put the platter down in front of him then backed away to the tent entrance. Zephyr reached out to take the meat but then stopped to speak, baffled how shy he suddenly was. "Thank you."

"You're welcome." Gawain's smile was blinding. "Eat. We have plenty."

Zephyr tried not to scarf the meat down but still ate fast. The shoulder bone in the meat snapped under his jaws, and Zephyr tossed the roast back, swallowing it nearly whole. He licked the platter clean before exhaustion hit him again, and he dropped his head to the pillows. Gawain took the platter away then came back.

The mage was with him, and a growl came out of his jaws before he could stop it. He pulled his wings in, but the wound on his wing made him hiss in pain, so he stopped.

"Easy, Zephyr," Gawain murmured, and the knight knelt beside him, one hand reaching out to catch the injured wing and lower it to the pillows. "Tristan won't hurt you. I won't let anyone hurt you."

Gawain's hands were so gentle, and his nerves tingled where they touched his scales. Zephyr stared at Gawain; his eyes as blue as the sky outside. They were earnest and kind, and Zephyr had learned at an early age how to spot evil in a man's eyes. A kind soul stared back at him, and a churring call rolled out from him. Gawain smiled wide and carefully sat on a cushion next to his shoulder.

"Tristan wants to help. Can we let him try?" Gawain asked him, and Zephyr eyed the mage.

"I just want to see if I can help," Tristan said, holding his hands out to the sides, fingers open, as if to show he had nothing hidden. He tilted his head toward the long gash in the wing joint, and Zephyr twitched. "I already helped the humans last night."

"I burned them," Zephyr whispered. He lowered his head and hid behind a pillow. "They tried to hurt me."

"I won't let them hurt you," Gawain promised. "Tristan won't either."

Zephyr grumbled but finally gave in. He wanted the pain to stop. He was defenseless anyway—if the mage wanted to hurt him, there was nothing Zephyr could do to stop him. He extended his wing, bumping Gawain in the back, and pain radiated down to his shoulder. He whimpered, and gentle hands cupped the injured joint.

"Easy, easy," Gawain said softly, soothing him. "Let me get out of the way, Tris, then you can get to work."

There was some shuffling, then Gawain was sitting next to his head. Zephyr came out from under the pillow, sniffing the man next to him. He focused on the knight and did his best not to run and hide when the mage knelt beside the injured wing.

They were very close to each other, yet Zephyr felt safe. Gawain was nice, and he spoke to Zephyr like a thinking being instead of an animal. He smelled like wonderful, clean scents, and there was no clinging odor of stress or pain or fear. The pleasing fragrance of the man with subtle underlays of horse, the clothing he wore, bread, and bacon filled his senses. Zephyr also detected fresh water from a cold stream and mutton tallow soap scented with pine along with a hint of castle-forged steel.

Zephyr jumped when the mage touched his wing, but there was no pain, just a prickling sensation and the rush of magic in the tent. Zephyr trembled, and he rested his head on Gawain's thigh without a thought. The firm muscles under his chin tensed for a second then slowly relaxed. A warm hand ran down the back of his neck, stroking the scales, and Zephyr churred, eyes drifting shut.

He floated in a happy, soft mental place, the petting soothing him in way that reminded him of being a youngling and coddled by his older nestmates. When the tingling along his wing intensified and hands held him still, he didn't panic as Gawain's hands brushed over his face, along his jaw, and satisfied an itch above his eye ridge. He pushed closer, and a surprised chuckle made him churr again.

"Is he asleep?"

"Dozing, I think. His wing?"

"I've closed the gash. He needs rest, food, and maybe another session. The marks to his lower legs need some attention. Should I do it now?"

Gawain rubbed his palm down the top of Zephyr's head. "Zephyr? Can Tris check your other wounds?"

If Gawain kept petting him, the mage could do whatever he liked. Zephyr butted his head under the knight's palm, demanding more touches. Gawain chuckled. "I think that's a yes. Go ahead."

The tingling returned, but Zephyr was too enchanted by the hands and the attention. He snuggled in deeper, head fully on the man's lap, and went limp, giving up his weight to the pillows. He could not recall the last time he ever felt so relaxed and free from worry or stress. Even as a youngling, before he and his family were captured and imprisoned, he never felt like this—safe and warm.

"I think he's fully asleep now," Gawain murmured. "I'm amazed he's letting me hold him like this."

There was a soft hum from the mage, as if he were thinking about something difficult. "He trusts you. He's been abused, and by the scarring, for a long time. I need to brush up on my research of dragons, but I think he's spent most, if not all, of his growing years in chains."

A hint of anger stirred the air, and Zephyr whimpered, but the hands soothed him back into his doze. "Is he fully grown?"

"He has the spikes of a full-grown dragon, despite the clipping done to them. Captivity and malnutrition have stunted his growth. I'd say he's still young but an adult. Dragons continue to grow for many years, even after they reach maturity, so with food and a safe place to live, he'll get bigger yet."

There was a beat of silence, then the mage spoke again, this time quieter, a bit urgent. "Gawain, he isn't a pet. You can't keep him."

"I know he isn't a pet, Tris." Gawain's reply was sharp, and it woke Zephyr from his doze. Zephyr grabbed onto the knight's waist and hugged him, curling in with his whole body. He put a wing along the man's back and all but crawled into his lap, blinking at the light from the midday sun. Gawain almost fell over but recovered, arms holding Zephyr around his shoulders and neck. Zephyr wound himself around the knight as much as he could and gently squeezed.

Zephyr rubbed his chin and jaw along the top of Gawain's head, the soft hair smelling of soap and man. A happy scent. He marked the human and used his tail to nudge the mage away.

"Mine," Zephyr said with a growl. Gawain gasped a bit but

didn't let him go, hugging him back. Zephyr glared at the mage, who was gaping at them, shocked. "Not a pet. I keep knight. My Gawain."

"All right, all right." Tristan held up his hands and scooted back before getting to his feet and heading for the tent entrance. "Your Gawain. I get it." Tristan cast a concerned glance to Gawain, but he left when Gawain shooed him out with a small wave.

❈ 6 ❈

A dragon the size of a warhorse climbing into his lap was not how Gawain expected his morning to go, but the heat radiating off the young dragon and the way Zephyr clung to him stifled any complaints he might have had. Zephyr was finally safe, and he needed to feel safe, so Gawain hugged as much of the dragon as he could and let him cling. Most of the dragon's weight was shifted to his hindquarters so thankfully it wasn't too much weight for Gawain's legs, but they wouldn't be able to stay as they were for more than a few minutes. Already his legs were stinging from restricted blood flow.

"It's all right," Gawain murmured, and Zephyr made that soft purring sound again, rubbing his jaw over Gawain's head and neck a few times. "What are you doing?"

"Smell good." Zephyr's voice was like music, a mix of deep baritone with a high tenor mixed together with some hissing on the vowels and soft clicks on the consonants. It was subtle, and he suspected that Zephyr could sound exactly like a human if he chose. "Mine. Smell like me now."

Gawain didn't understand, but the change in Zephyr

36

overnight was encouraging. The injuries were healed, though Zephyr would need some time to recover and grow stronger. The open wounds on his legs were now faded marks, the scales growing anew. "Do you feel better?"

"Yesss." Long and drawn out, Gawain was reminded of a snake or a cat, but a part of him was amused at his mind trying to compare the dragon in his lap to any other creature. Zephyr was all dragon, as the hint of fire and smoke in the tent along with the scrape of scales over linen and silk covered pillows proved. Heat poured off Zephyr's lithe form that made it impossible for him to deny the truth—he was hugging a dragon who was doing his best to scent mark him and was coiled around him possessively.

A horse neighed outside the tent, and he heard snippets of conversation through the walls. He needed to get geared up to go into the village and talk to the townsfolk, but it could wait for a bit. "Zephyr? Can I ask you some questions?"

A soft churr was his answer, and he nudged at the dragon until Zephyr moved off his lap. He straightened out his legs with a relieved groan. Zephyr tilted his head, one large ember-colored eye blinking slowly at him, level with his head. From running his hands over them while Tristan worked, he knew the scales around Zephyr's eyes were softer than the rest of him, though the hide was tough and thick, and many of the scales were rough to the touch.

"Ask." Zephyr reached out and nudged the closest hand, and Gawain went back to petting the ridge over that perfect eye, down the long skull, and to the spikes that were crudely clipped. He imagined the dark brown spikes were several inches longer in their natural state. "You escaped from someplace bad. Did you escape alone?" If there were more dragons out in the woods, they needed to be found, for everyone's safety.

"Alone." The reply was a whisper, and his chest ached in sympathy for the loneliness he heard underneath.

"Who did you escape from?" Zephyr went to hide his head under a pillow, but Gawain caught the formidable jaws, cupping the dragon's chin and lifting his head back up. Zephyr was far stronger but let him get away with it. "Are they coming after you?"

THE QUESTION WAS A SHOCK AND FEAR RACED ALONG HIS nerves, his spikes twitching. The hands holding his head were steady and refused to let him hide. Zephyr wanted to run and keep running until he was so lost in the world no one could find him, but Gawain was a shining beacon in an otherwise confusing jumble of sights and sounds.

A golden glow covered the knight, shimmering with each beat of his heart. Zephyr blinked and looked again, this time deeper. The glow grew stronger, more intense, until he let the focus slip away and looked upon the surface again.

His magic was returning. The knight's aura was a shroud of golden mist that flowed and ebbed with the lifeforce that emanated out from his body. Subtle streams of silver accented the gold of the aura, and the colors were enough for Zephyr to trust him completely. There were no dark, muddied rivers of virulent oranges or angry reds, none of the colors he associated with malice or a corrupted soul. Gawain was so different from the mage that once enslaved Zephyr that any hesitancy he instinctively held evaporated like mist under the morning sun.

"A mage," Zephyr answered. "Chained me, took me from the nest I was born in, my broodmother too."

Gawain's expression was calm, but his scent held threads of anger. His aura remained steady, reaffirming Zephyr's conclusion that Gawain was a good man. Gawain stroked the scales on his cheek. "Is your broodmother still held captive?"

Zephyr looked down, a quiet whimper slipping out. "No. Gone now, many years." His broodmother died in chains, deep in the dungeons beneath the mage's castle. Her magic exhausted, and her strength reduced to a shadow of what it once was by the lack of movement and open skies. She encouraged him to fly as best he could before he grew too big for their stone cell.

"I'm sorry." Compassion and sympathy laced the words. "Do you know where this was? And is this mage going to come after you?"

"Don't know. Flamed him when the guards changed my collar." The guards had come to put a new collar on him, as he had grown into the old one and the metal was warping. Bespelled to keep him compliant, the shackles only worked while they were intact, and they needed to be changed out before a growth spurt damaged the spells etched into the collars.

Zephyr hesitantly shared the tale of how he escaped. Pure luck and human error. The guards hadn't seen him in person for several months, instead throwing food through the grate in the door into the large room carved into the bedrock beneath the castle. The equestrian staircase that once allowed mounted riders into the heart of the keep was closed and welded shut by spells. The only way in or out of the former stables turned into a cage he'd spent years in was a large grate at the opposite side of the space from the wide staircase. The grated passage led upward into the castle and was how the mage came down to steal his magic once it had replenished enough from the last culling. Over the years, the guards had changed, but the last pair had been there for two growth cycles and had become his guards just after the death of his mother. Complacent and thinking him a tamed animal, they ignored him. They hadn't looked closely at his collar or the shackles about his legs for months, and the one on his rear leg had snapped and fallen off without their notice.

When they'd cautiously entered the cage, Zephyr didn't react, and eventually the guards relaxed, thinking him cowed. For years he'd fought and snapped and tried to escape when the shackles were changed or the guards trimmed his claws and spikes with their cruel tools. Yet there he lay, remaining still, not reacting, so as they went back and forth between the place the chains and shackles were stored and his cage, they didn't alert the mage as to what they were doing. When one guard unclipped the collar while the other went out to drag in the new set, Zephyr had struck.

"I killed the one who took off my collar," he said. "I bit his neck and shoulder, he died quickly. I burnt to ash the guard who came in when he heard the first one scream."

Gawain listened, not speaking, his aura showing patience and concern.

"My fire returned because the collar was not on my neck. I melted the shackles and ran up the ramp, the one they had dragged me through as an eggling. I flamed the doors for so long the iron caught fire and ran red down the ramp." Zephyr paused and looked out of the tent. The grass was green, and a soft cool breeze played with the fabric tied back at the sides of the doorway. The sun was bright, and the pieces of the sky he could see through the trees were a brilliant blue. He was free. He'd made it out. "I don't know if other guards summoned the mage or if he felt his spells fall—he came to stop me just as the iron doors to the outside ran like water and the ground began to burn."

"You got away."

"Yessss." Zephyr closed his eyes and leaned into the knight. "He cast at me, screaming, angry. I spun and flamed him. I used my magic to make it burn hotter, hotter than flame can burn alone, and when I saw nothing but smoke and darkness, I ran outside."

"Did you kill him? Do you think he's dead?"

"Don't know. I used much of my magic to burn so hot then more to make myself strong enough to fly over the mountains. I hurt my wing running out of the stones falling from where the doors once were and flying made it worse. I landed once I got past the tallest peaks. No magic left, could not fly."

The trip over the mountains wasn't planned. He hadn't flown once he grew too big for the dungeons, and his wings weren't strong enough without his magic assisting. Functioning almost entirely on instinct and half-remembered lessons from his broodmother before she died, he made it work out of sheer desperation. He took to the air as soon as he saw the sky and didn't stop for anything.

"Do you know the mage's name?" Gawain's question was enough to make him jerk, and he tried to hide his face, shivering. "Easy, easy. I'm sorry. I only ask in case he comes looking for you. Knowing his name can help us keep you safe."

"Do not know his name. Know his voice, his face, his scent. But not a name." Zephyr sighed heavily, ribs stretching as he sucked in a deep breath.

It felt so good to be able to stretch out, no chains weighing him down. His pains were all but gone, and he'd been fed. He thought he was full until his belly rumbled loud enough for the human to hear.

Gawain laughed. "I think you need some more food. I can fetch you some." Gawain climbed out of the nest of pillows and got to his feet. "Unless you want to come out with me? My knights won't hurt you."

Zephyr watched as the sunlight behind Gawain lit his hair in a halo, a nimbus of gold that matched the knight's aura. He blinked back the magic and focused on the man, climbing to his feet as well. The scrapes and scars on his ankles and wrists were nearly gone, though the scales bore silver scars and the hide felt tender. He brought the injured wing forward and examined the joint—the muscles were whole, the hide in one piece, and his scales shone with a healthy glimmer. No sign of an injury but for a thin silver line along the largest muscle over the bend in the joint. Zephyr did not feel fully strong again, but far stronger than he had in a very long time. His magic was returning, faster than ever before—the mage was no longer there to drain it away from him as it returned, and he was grown now. More magic, and without the chains and collars, it was his to control as he wished.

"I come." Zephyr stretched out, claws scratching over the floor of the tent, and he hastily pulled back his tail before he destroyed the back wall of the structure.

Gawain led the way out, and Zephyr followed. He stood up to his full height, and on four feet, he was a head taller than the knight. No crawling for him anymore. Standing so tall, without hitting his head on the stone ceiling of his cell, was bliss.

A horse whinnied and stamped, and the humans in the camp all paused in their tasks and looked toward Gawain and Zephyr. He ducked into a half crouch and slinked until his head was behind the knight's back. Gawain twisted and looked down at him with a smile on his face. "They can still see you."

"I can't see them."

"Ahh," Gawain breathed as if he understood. Maybe he did. His knight was smart. "Come with me." Gawain took off slowly, heading for a fire surrounded by stones with an iron tripod over the center holding a metal pot, and along the edge, an iron spit was set aside with a huge chunk of meat slowly cooking, fats dripping into a shallow dish underneath it on the edge of the coals. A table was set up nearby, and a young human female was hacking at chunks of red meat with an odd, heavy-looking knife that hit with a solid thunk when it cut through the meat and hit the wood of the table. Another young female human was tending the fire, and an older female, this one with bared arms and muscles much like Gawain's, sat next to the spit, flipping ash out of the drippings with a thin stick and eyeing the roast as it slowly cooked. The older female was darker in color than the younger ones, her skin a gleaming copper with brown undertones. A few scars dotted her arms, thin lines like slashes from a beast, but they were neat and not ragged like they would be from an animal attack.

The strong, mature female glanced at Zephyr, and he ducked behind Gawain again, taking swift peeks over his knight's shoulder when they reached the fire. "Avril, this is Zephyr. Zephyr, Avril is one of my knights, and she's going to help me keep you safe. The squire cutting our supper over there is Mel, and the squire minding the fire is Ari." Zephyr peeked, and the squire with the knife waved at him and held up a piece of meat.

"Go on," Gawain said softly, and Zephyr took a couple halting steps toward the squire. He reached out, his long neck nearly straight, and she tossed it to him with a flick of her

43

wrist. He caught the chunk of meat and chewed on it, happy to discover it was a section of rib bones covered in strips of meat. It crunched loudly as he crushed the bones in his jaws, and he tossed it back and swallowed. He looked hopefully at the squire, the one Gawain named Mel.

"Think ye want the bones then, yeah?" Mel asked, and even before he could reply, she reached down and grabbed a long bone with a meaty joint on the end. "Most predators need bone in their meals. 'Ere's the leg bone. Too big for the stew pot. All yours."

She threw it over the table, and Zephyr snapped it out of the air, then he sank down beside the fire with his treat. He looked at Gawain, who arched a brow at him, and Zephyr turned back to the squire. "Thank youuss." The last word hissed a bit, but she understood, waving him off as she got back to work.

The meat was still fresh, blood dripping from the bone and the joint, and Zephyr licked at it before taking a deep breath and slowly exhaling on his prize. Stirring up flame that wasn't meant to go farther than the front of his nose was tough to manage, but he got a few licks of fire out. The meat blackened and crisped, fat snapping. He held the long bone in his front paws and chewed on the end, watching the humans. The female sitting across the fire pit watched him warily, no doubt having seen him char the meat, but she didn't smell of fear; her aura was calm and steady, a mix of rainbow hues. There was wary respect in her gaze before she looked away and spoke quietly to the female chopping meat.

A pair of male humans were near the horses, who Zephyr thought might be tasty, but even he knew that the horses were prized by the humans and worth more alive and working than as a meal. His mother told him stories about the wider world during their captivity, and while he had been young when captured, he'd seen some of the world of men before that horrible day. Not much, and it was a mess of distant recollections, but it was enough to ground him.

Gawain sat on a rock near the fire, and Zephyr wanted to crawl into this lap and share the meat, but humans cooked their food with more than a surface char. Seemed silly to him, but the smells from the pot over the fire were yummy. He compromised and put his tail very carefully beside the knight where he sat. He had spikes on his tail tip, and while the ends were blunted, he could still hurt the human by accident. He continued to eat and pretended not to notice when Gawain shot him a narrowed-eyed glance when he slipped his tail right up against his thigh and left it there. Even that much contact soothed the need to crawl into Gawain's lap and never leave. He was too big in his current form to do it safely without squishing his human. Maybe when his magic returned he could try it.

"What's the plan for the day?" The knight named Avril asked. She smelled like metal, horses, leather, and a bit of magic. Zephyr kept eating but looked past the surface at her aura, and it sang with a rainbow of bright colors. She was mageborn, but not to the same level as the one called Tristan. She could do minor things and, unless she caught him sleeping, was not a threat to Zephyr magically. He would watch her, but she didn't feel threatening, not like the mage who captured him and his mother.

Gawain sent him a searching glance before responding. "I need to go to the village and talk to the elders. Then I guess it depends on Zephyr after that."

Zephyr didn't understand, so he kept eating, gnawing on the bone and snapping off pieces. He sucked out the marrow then swallowed the bone fragments.

Later that day saw him returning from the village back to his camp. Gawain lightly kicked his mount's sides, urging the stallion into a canter. The meeting in the village went longer than he wanted, and despite Evern showing up with the problem bear's corpse strung over his horse's back and gold from the queen's purse going to the affected farmers and hunters, the villagers were too angry and suspicious. Though scars would remain, the hunters were healed by Tristan. None of them were maimed permanently.

Zephyr would not be safe in Morvain. And unless Zephyr was accompanied by knights, other humans were likely to react as the villagers had—with violence and suspicion. The chronicles that told of dragons being thinking and rational creatures were considered myth and fantasy in the outer reaches of the kingdom, and despite Gawain's reassurances that Zephyr was no threat as long as he was left alone, his promises were met with stone-cold stubbornness and doubt.

Evern matched his pace, the older knight appearing none the worse for wear despite his long night and even longer day. Evern was stationed at a village a day's ride back toward the capital and would not be staying either. The queen's knights had given refuge to the dragon the villagers wanted dead— some time and distance might be best for the village of Morvain.

Tristan rode behind them by a few lengths, not in any rush, the mage casting his gyrfalcon out into the trees for his supper. Tristan was the only one of their party who received a warm welcome from the village, his healing abilities and his presence doing much to calm tempers. Gawain's royal status and titles only made the villagers resentful, likely due to him barring their way to Zephyr. Tristan was good for a distraction, and the handsome mage with his gold blond hair and charming smile was enough to soften even the hardest of hearts. The villagers spent most of the long day avoiding the knights and hovering around Tristan.

They made it back to camp in short order, slowing to a walk as the road gave way to grass and the old trees of the orchard spread out above them. Evern reined in his gelding and dismounted, and Gawain did the same. The camp was visible through the evenly spaced out trees with the wagons in the next row covered with rough cloths. They would not be extending their stay, and Gawain was occupied with thoughts of Zephyr. The dragon fell asleep not long after eating, curled up on the pillows in Gawain's tent. He hadn't even managed to sleep in his own tent yet and was looking forward to resting that night.

"I have not seen you for months, my prince," Evern spoke quietly. "You look well."

Gawain sent Evern a searching glance, but the older knight looked ahead, giving away nothing. "I thought I said not to call me that." Gawain smiled a bit, teasing. "And for a man who wanted an easy posting, you've been rather busy."

Evern chuckled and cast him a sharp glance. "I wasn't expecting homicidal villagers and a rambunctious dragon.

And hunting an angry bear that's eating livestock wasn't part of my plans when I asked for an easy post." Evern gestured back over his shoulder toward Tristan, whose mount was at an amble back on the road, the mage staring off into the woods. "Your cousin told me the young dragon spent most of the morning curled in your lap and scent-marking you."

"Hhmm." He had nothing to say, not really. He wasn't upset at all that Zephyr appeared to be staking a claim. There were worse things out in the world than a possessive dragon. Maybe. "We've kept him safe, and I think he's had precious little of that. He may relax once he grows more secure."

Evern snorted and shook his head. "Or you'll end up in a dragon's hoard."

"There's worse places to be, I'm sure," Gawain retorted. There was no chance the young dragon would be as zealous in his adoration once he found a place to belong and some security.

Jon, the youngest squire of the three, came jogging over once they reached the camp and took their mounts. Gawain unhooked his sheathed sword from the saddle and carried it to his tent. Jon tugged the warhorses away, chattering happily to the steeds, who snorted back. Jon tended to spoil them with dried apple bits and scratches. Evern headed for the fire and the pot staying warm over the coals.

Avril and Bedivere stood talking in front of their tent, and he lifted a hand in greeting as he passed but didn't stop. "Briefing in an hour." They nodded in response and went back to their quiet conversation.

The flap was down over the entrance to his tent, and he carefully opened it a few inches to look inside. The smoke vent at the top was peeled back, letting in the sun, and he smiled at the dragon sleeping on his pillows. He usually bunked with Tristan when they were on campaign together, his cousin sharing his tent, but with the dragon's wariness around mages, Tristan was bunking with Felix and Axton. The night before Gawain hadn't slept much at all—he spent the night sitting by the fire in the middle of their camp, watching the woods past the orchard and thinking about what to do.

Gawain slid inside and let the flap fall closed behind him. He carefully made his way across his tent and put his sword on the rack designed to hold his gear. They hadn't even had time to unload the wagons fully—their mission was completed within hours of reaching Morvain. He was thankful for that—it meant Zephyr wasn't alone, injured, and at risk of dying along with the mob of angry villagers while Gawain and his knights scoured the countryside.

A single chest for clothing and his unused portable bed box in its chest were unloaded, and his dragon guest would have never fit upon it if it was in use. It served well enough as a bench, and he sat to tug off his boots. His sleeping pillows made for a decent enough bed, and the ground wasn't as cold as it could have been if they'd made this trip out even a week earlier. The bespelled wax cloth underneath the rugs kept everything dry and any early spring bugs out.

Zephyr didn't wake, though he twitched a bit, and a soft whimper slipped out. Gawain went to the dragon, and gently, so as not to wake him, slid a hand down the back of his head and along the nape of his neck, stopping at the first large spike. Zephyr sighed and yawned, then snuggled down deeper in to the pillows. The young dragon needed all the sleep he could get to recover fully.

Gawain sat on a free pillow and rubbed his face. He needed a nap. That was the last thing he remembered before sliding down and cracking a yawn, falling asleep in moments to the sound of a dragon breathing next to him.

Zephyr snuffled then stretched, remembering that the tent was there just before he punched a hole through it with his tail. Opening his eyes, he was happy to see his knight with him on the pillows, sleeping. Gawain had rolled to his side and had one hand outstretched, fingers touching one of his paws. Gawain smelled of contentment. It was a subtle scent that made his scales shiver.

Zephyr stood, heading for the tent entrance and nosing underneath the flap so he could leave. Careful with his tail, he got stuck when his wings got mired in the fabric, and it took a few hops to free himself. He spun, tugging his tail free, and looked around. He needed the trees for a bit.

A few humans blinked at him in shock, but they made no aggressive moves, and the older female named Avril walked over to him, stopping a cautious distance away. Though if he wanted to attack her, she was far too close. He didn't though, and she somehow knew that. Her magic lay quiet, and he sensed no threat from her.

"Can I help you with something, Zephyr?"

Zephyr shuffled, scoring the earth and grass with a hind paw as he tried to formulate an answer. She stared at him for a moment before smiling at him. He tilted his head and chirped. She grinned wide then pointed across the camp, opposite of where the horses were being kept. "We dug a ditch just past the last row of trees in the orchard before it grows wild again. Don't stray too far, please. I don't want the villagers to try and hurt you again."

"Thankssss." He ducked his head and walked slowly through the camp, keeping his tail low and holding in the urge to let it sway and twitch with his mood. He didn't want to knock anyone over or destroy a tent. Once he cleared the camp, he followed his nose, though he wouldn't use the ditch. He snorted to clear the smell then headed a short distance upwind and slid into the woods. He took care of his needs and used a sliver of magic to clean himself for the first time in a very long time. When kept in the dungeons, he couldn't use his magic for grooming, and he relished in the chance now.

From tail tip to the end of his nose, he shivered again, and magic bloomed in the air around him, removing grime, blood, dirt, and dead layers of scales and hide. He shook himself out, letting his nerves calm down, then he stretched long and hard, scratching the ground and scoring a tree, enjoying the tug on his claws and each knuckle. He headed back to camp at a slow amble, sniffing the breeze and parsing the scents, eyes and ears deciphering each sound and movement.

"Zephyr?" Gawain's call floated through the trees and his heart kicked up. Gawain sounded worried, so he sprinted for the camp.

He barreled into the camp and skidded to a halt at Gawain's feet, the knight backing up a step before laughing. Zephyr sniffed his knight all over and butted his head on the man's shoulder. He appeared to be well. "Was fine. Gawain worriesss?"

Gawain nodded. "I was worried, but you're here now. Time to talk to the others and find out what we're doing."

Zephyr hissed out a happy breath through his fangs and shadowed Gawain as he went toward the group of knights and their servants. The squires were clustered together and whispering, and there was a new knight who was standing very close to the young knight called Axton. They smelled of heat and fresh sweat, and their heart rates were faster and faces slightly flushed. He tilted his head and stared, and when the younger knight shuffled closer to the older knight and the more mature male put a hand on the younger's hip, realization came. Mates. Mating was something Zephyr had never experienced himself but remembered witnessing as a youngling. Sex and mating were never hidden among his kind, and the pursuit of younglings wasn't the only motivation for dragons to mate.

"Since Zephyr is the only dragon in the area, and the situation with the bear is resolved, it's time to leave. I'm going to advise the Queen to increase patrols in the area and increase communication between border towns and the rest of the kingdom. This isolation is increasing the chances for miscommunication and xenophobia that will spill over into violence, as we've seen already." Gawain spoke to his people, and the humans all watched him and some nodded, others just listening and waiting. Gawain was the leader, and his words were important. "We'll be heading back to the capital tomorrow so tensions can dissipate. Zephyr, will you come with us?"

Zephyr stopped examining the way Gawain's long hair caught on his trimmed beard and blinked at him "Yessss? Go where?" He might not have been paying attention.

Gawain smiled at him, and Zephyr churred, rubbing his jaw along the man's shoulder. "Come back to the capital with us? My sister is the Queen, the ruler of these lands, and she'd love to meet you. You will be safe with us and have a place to recover and decide what you want to do now that you're free."

"I will stay with my Gawain?" Zephyr would go with Gawain, no matter what the dominant female of their people wanted, but it would be easier if Gawain thought it was his idea. She would say yes if her nestmate was happy. The other humans snorted or laughed, breaking off into coughs or biting their lips, watching in amusement. Gawain arched a dark brow at his people before turning to Zephyr.

"If you want, I can help you settle in. There will be a lot of other humans, and some may fear you, but you can stay at the castle and be safe. I promise I'll keep you safe."

Gawain wanted him to stay. Zephyr hummed and a stream of smoke escaped his nostrils and floated up to the sky. He was happy. "I will go with you."

8

A night spent sleeping on pillows instead of his bedroll, with a dragon curled around him like a giant house cat was a new experience, but he woke rested and ready to meet the day. Waking with his head pillowed on a leg that was covered in scales, a long-fingered, hand-like paw capped in black claws coming into focus as he rubbed sleep from his eyes, was a bit strange, but the comfort and warmth in the pile of pillows erased the faint unease. Zephyr cracked an ember eye at him when Gawain sat up, stretching. Zephyr watched him with something akin to fondness, and the dragon's evident affection for him made Gawain ache a bit under his ribs. Zephyr had him partially covered by his now-healed wing, and Gawain gave the dragon a soft smile when he pulled his wing back and let in the cool morning air.

"Good morning," Gawain said, stretching his arms over his head, loose tunic riding up his abdomen.

Zephyr grumbled, a deep and content purr of sound. He reached out with his snout and rubbed his nose along the ridges of Gawain's belly, and he laughed, gently nudging the inquisitive dragon away with his hands. Zephyr tilted his head to the side and puffed out a tiny smoke ring, slow blinking in lazy drowsiness. "Good morning, Gawain. Smell good."

"I smell good?" Gawain asked, mildly incredulous. He hadn't bathed since their last day in an inn on their way to Morvain, and that was days ago. A dosing from a couple of jugs of hot water and a quick scrub with a clean rag since then but not a full bath, and he smelled like sweat and horse and smoke. And dragon, though the scent of Zephyr was pleasant and reminded him of quiet evenings before a crackling hearth and a goblet of red wine. "I need a bath. There's a river along the road back to the capital, I can get a thorough wash in then. Come, it's time to get up. We have to break down camp then get on the road."

"Food?" Zephyr asked hopefully. Gawain crawled out of the pillow pile, opened the tent flap over the entrance, and saw a haunch of meat cooking over the fire.

"Avril has your breakfast." Gawain gestured, tying up the flap and stepping out of the tent. A wooden bowl piled high with round meat pies the size of his palm waited beside the fire on a rock. The rest of the retinue were up already, half the tents broken down. It looked like they'd let them sleep in for as long as they could, and Gawain appreciated it. Zephyr needed the rest.

Zephyr went for the meat cooking, and Gawain followed, taking a small loaf of warm bread stuffed with cheese and a cup of spell-cleaned water from Avril with gratitude. She helped Zephyr pull the meat off the iron bar, then went about putting out the fire. Gawain ate fast then handed off the cup to Mel and Jon, the squires working quickly and efficiently, and the rest of the retinue going about their tasks with similar efficacy.

Camp broke down in less than an hour; the wagons were hitched, and the warhorses saddled. Tristan was casting off his gyrfalcon as Zephyr watched with avid interest, though Gawain was very grateful they'd explained the bird was a treasured companion and not something to eat. Zephyr took it in stride and didn't seem troubled by it, and even sniffed the wary bird with a hello before laying down and watching them break camp.

Tristan approached after sending the bird aloft. "I've sent him ahead with some notices to the villages on the road back to the capital, so people aren't terrified when we ride through town with a dragon."

"Good idea," Gawain said as he took the reins to his steed, Mel dashing off afterward to double check nothing was lost in the grass. "I don't want people to panic. We may need to camp along the road and not in a village on the first couple of nights. It won't be possible the last night before we hit the city limits, but we can always get a late start the second day and ride through the night so we can come in during darkness. I don't see how we can alert the city guard and keep people from mobbing us for a look at a dragon within the city."

"We'll have to figure it out, but I sent word ahead to Elise as well. She may send soldiers out to meets us. I'll watch for a return message."

Tristan could send messages ahead to other mages who worked for the crown and alert the queen of pressing matters, but it required a great deal of preparation and wasn't something Tristan could do from horseback. The gyrfalcon was equipped with energy and spells to assist it in flying faster, farther, and for longer periods of time in order to drop off messages at designated spots within each major village along their route back to the city. The raptor carried spells for protection from weather; energy loss, so it didn't need to hunt; and protection from predators, weapons, and accidents. It was complicated and took concentration for Tristan to weave it all together.

There were other means of communication, such as a messenger on horseback or pigeons carrying small missives, but the raptor was the easiest, and through the connection Tristan had with the bird, he was able to determine exactly when a message was delivered, if the right person got it, and if it was read. Tristan could see and hear through the bond, and the spells kept the bird safe and healthy as it flew on its own across the country.

His horse snorted and danced to the side, almost knocking him on his ass. Zephyr was eye to eye with the horse, who settled down after a minute. "Easy, Zephyr. Don't scare the horse, please."

"Sorrrry." Zephyr backed up a bit, eyeing the warhorse. "You ride him."

"Um, yes?"

"I am big as the horse." Zephyr was the same size, sort of, and three times as long. He was recovering nicely, and his ribs weren't as prominent as they had been. He was lean, muscled, and looked terrifying, and he was clearly a predator. His chest was heavily muscled and deep, and his shoulders where the wings met his back were even more defined than his chest muscles. His scales were intense in color—the shades of fire and sunlight mixed with black as dark and shiny as a raven's wing. With some more food in him, Zephyr would be an absolute powerhouse, and that wasn't even seeing him fly yet.

"Yes, you're big like my horse. Fierce and handsome too."

Zephyr was a stunning being, and Gawain was pleased to see the dragon preen a bit at the compliment, arching his long neck and blinking at him with ember-colored eyes. "Gawain mine."

Tristan smirked at him. Gawain nodded slowly, wondering where Zephyr was going. "Sure?"

Zephyr shifted on his clawed feet and flicked his wings before settling. "Gawain not ride horse." Zephyr pushed his snout out and blinked at Gawain slowly. "Gawain mine. I will carry Gawain."

His mouth dropped open, and he gaped. Tristan was equally shocked and just stared at the young dragon. He tried to speak but failed. He coughed then tried again. "What?"

Zephyr huffed, growing impatient. "Gawain mine. I will carry Gawain. Not horse."

He might be able to straddle the point on the dragon's back in front of the wings and after the last spike on his neck, but Zephyr wasn't built like a horse with the wide barrel rib cage and the breeding to carry a full-grown knight in armor for long periods of time. "Thank you, Zephyr. I would love to one day. But you're still recovering, and I don't want to take advantage of you. You're not an animal, and I don't want people to see me riding you and think that you're to be treated like a horse."

"I am strong. Not a horse. Dragon. I look nothing like a horse." Zephyr was confused, and Gawain was worried he'd offended him.

"One day, when you're better and if you still want to, I'd

love to go for a ride. But our horses are bred and raised for the purpose of carrying knights, and I don't want to hurt you or make you uncomfortable. I am honored by the offer, though. Please don't think I don't want to—I just don't want to hurt you." Zephyr might be able to carry his weight for a few minutes now, but not for a three-day journey back to the capital.

Zephyr grumbled and one front paw grabbed at the grass and tore it up in clumps in a distracted manner as he squinted at the horse. The steed was a steady and dependable sort, so it ignored the large unhappy predator as best it could.

"I think about thisssss." Zephyr drew out the last word and gave Gawain a disgruntled flick of his wings. "Gawain mine."

Zephyr was upset, and that bothered him. He hurried to reassure Zephyr, not wanting the dragon to be sad or hurt by his refusal. "Yes, I'm yours." If Zephyr needed to claim Gawain to feel safe, then he'd just have to belong to the dragon.

"Be careful," Tristan murmured. "You shouldn't indulge him until you know what he means by that."

"Gawain mine!" Zephyr declared loudly, and the horse snorted, tossing his head. Zephyr shrank down, eyeing the horse, seeming to realize he'd scared it. "Sssorry."

The walking was tiring. They'd been walking all day, the road empty of travelers, and the sun was setting, the wind picking up. He did not smell rain, not yet, just cold winds coming down into the lower elevations as the day changed into night. Zephyr whimpered, and he sat in the middle of the road, ready to stop. He was stopping and not going another step. He dropped and laid himself in the dirt and gave a huge exhale, leg muscles burning from the exercise.

His knight dismounted and walked back to him before crouching and meeting him at eye level. "Tired?"

"Yesss," Zephyr hissed out, the exhale strong enough he raised up a burst of dust from the gravel road.

Gawain chuckled. "Not used to walking this much, huh? We can stop for the night." Gawain peered up at the sky, his long hair whipping about as the wind increased with a burst of cold before subsiding. "The weather looks like it might turn. We're done for the day." Gawain stood and whistled loudly. His knights drew to a halt further down the road, and Gawain did a strange wave at them. The retinue headed off the road onto a wide flat grass field that ended at the treeline. "Come on. Don't rest in the road. Grass is nicer."

Zephyr grumbled but got to his feet and slowly followed Gawain off the road and out into the field. The wagons behind them pulled along the side of the road, and the squires hurried about tending to the horses. The wind pulled at the cloths covering the wagons, and the horses stamped restlessly.

Zephyr followed on Gawain's heels, and when the knight tied his horse off to a tree branch, Zephyr lay in the grass beside the warhorse and watched as the humans moved to set up camp. The other knights did the same with their horses, and while one of the squires started at the first horse and began tending to the steed, undoing straps and harnesses, the knights headed for the wagons.

One of the squires grabbed a leather strap that was as long as he was tall and a hatchet before heading into the trees. The sun was about an hour from setting, but dark clouds gilded in orange fire with ominous black underbellies obscured the light. The clouds were moving fast and would soon be gone, but the chance for rain pushed the humans to work faster.

The squire returned with the strap wrapped around tree branches in a bundle, then he released it, letting the wood fall before he jogged back into the trees with the strap and hatchet.

Watching the humans set up their camp was entertaining, and Zephyr relaxed. The air was growing heavy with moisture, and a few drops of rain landed on his wings, but a downpour wasn't about to hit. They might catch the tail end of the storm as it raced away.

Zephyr eyed the warhorse when the squire finally reached Gawain's mount. The horse was tall and heavily muscled, a dark brown color that made him think of damp earth beneath leaves. Big hooves, a thick arching neck, big head, and a wide sturdy back meant for carrying humans, the horse couldn't be more different than a dragon. Zephyr got up and out of the way as the squire worked, though he watched the horse, wondering how it would feel to carry Gawain on his back.

His magic was returning, but he was not sure if he could manage a full transformation. He was stronger, and growing more so the longer he enjoyed his freedom, but recovering from years of captivity wasn't something he could fix with magic. A few more days and his magic might be back to normal, though it had been so long since his magic wasn't culled from him that he was unsure. Maybe Gawain would go riding with him if he were shaped like a horse. The first creature he transformed into when he was an eggling was far smaller, a crow, and his broodmother reprimanded him and made him change back before he got stuck. Transforming his shape at such a young age was not wise, considering his lack of focus and the erratic nature of his magic. Of course, he'd continued to practice when she wasn't watching him and managed to transform into a deer. His scales remained in odd patches and the fur was uneven, but he had done it. The crow was easier as it was closer to his size and had wings. More practice would have resolved those problems eventually.

If he could manage to transform, to shapeshift into another animal, he could then return to his primary form and regain lost muscle mass and stamina from the years in chains. It wouldn't be permanent, but he could manage it for a short while if he built up his magical reserves.

Gawain was nearby, tending to the sidebags the squire had removed from the horse. The female knights were hacking at the grass, cutting away a circle of it that they put to the side then stacking wood in the area of exposed damp earth. The squire came back with another bundle before darting back for the trees.

The wind picked up again, short strong bursts that caught at the tents the retinue were hurriedly trying to get up. The temperature was dropping, and while it didn't bother Zephyr, the humans were susceptible to the cold and damp. Zephyr got to his feet, slowly stretching out his stiffening muscles, then padded over the pile of sticks in the bared area of earth. Avril was reaching out and tapping at the wood, her magic rousing enough to call fire, but the wind kicked the tiny flames and put them out. "We may not have a fire tonight if this wind keeps up."

Zephyr sat with his back to the wind and unfurled his wings, the wind pushing against the backside of them, buffeting him with short but intense bursts. His wings blocked enough of it that the immediate space around the unlit campfire calmed. Craning his neck down, he parted his jaws and breathed out slowly and gently over the pile of wood. Heat wavered in the air, then the wood darkened, and smoke twirled up into the air in thin tendrils before the wood caught fire with a soft whoosh.

The fire crackled, and flames reached for the sky. Avril chuckled. "Thank you. You're handy on the road, aren't you?"

Zephyr preened a bit, and Avril laughed. She went to work making supper for the humans, and Zephyr sniffed in appreciation when she got a bespelled leather pouch that when opened released the scent of raw meat and blood. The meat was preserved in the pouch, and kept from spoiling, smelling of cold air and faint hints of other foodstuffs from past use, though nothing rotten. Just hints of odors that mingled with the meat and made him salivate.

A few more pouches and food was cooking for everyone, and Avril brushed her hands together as she stood and stretched. Her tunic even out in front, the fabric falling straight, and Zephyr made out a stylized image of a dragon in flight. He blinked then looked at the rest of the humans. The people who weren't knights had patches on their shoulders or upper arms of the same image, though not as finely detailed. The knights had tunics of varying cuts and styles, and in the case of the mage, robes and a long tunic slit on the sides, but all of them had the same image.

"Dragons." Zephyr tilted his head and pointed with a claw at the image on Avril's tunic. She looked confused for a second then glanced down and smoothed out the fabric.

"Ahh. Yes, it's a dragon in flight, the sigil of the Royal House of Kentaine. We wear the sigil since we are Sir Gawain's knights, under his personal command. Our retinue wears the same symbol, though not so prominently displayed."

Zephyr churred softly, thinking. He snuck a glance at Gawain, the knight helping a squire set up a tent. It was smaller than the ones they'd used back at Morvain, the waxed hemp sides stiffer and probably rain repellent. The wind kicked at the tent, but Tristan came to assist. Zephyr felt magic stir, and the tent lifted itself and settled into place in defiance to the wind. They repeated this a few more times until a handful of tents were assembled.

While he was watching, the humans finally finished setting up the camp, and a second fire was coaxed to life not far from where the horses were tied off. Not for warmth—to keep predators at bay. It wouldn't deter a dragon, but it would keep a mountain cat or wolf at a distance. Two of the servants set up at that fire, and the humans discussed a schedule for keeping watch through the night. Gawain and Tristan were given the last watch, a couple hours before dawn, and Zephyr followed Gawain into his tent after the humans ate.

Though smaller than the tent they first shared, Zephyr still fit within the waterproof tent. He lay curled upon the sleeping pillows, and Gawain rested in the curve of his body, head pillowed on Zephyr's shoulder. A thin blanket covered Gawain, though it had slipped down and revealed the naked torso of the knight, pooling about his hips. Gawain wore braies of soft cotton, and Zephyr enjoyed the smooth warm skin and pleasant scent of the human resting against him. A wing lay over Gawain protectively, keeping faint drafts that slipped through the tent and the dampness in the night air at bay. It rained not long after they bedded down, and while it didn't last long, it was enough to add a sharp chill to the air.

Zephyr woke sometime in the middle of the night, senses alert. He could hear the horses, somewhat restless, a few snorting and blowing hard. The night was quiet aside from the horses.

Too quiet.

No night birds or insects called, the wind was silent, and the faint snap of wood burning in the campfire echoed loudly in the unnatural quiet. A horse snorted loudly and stamped a foot, and Zephyr extended his senses, listening for what bothered the animals.

Footsteps. Stealthy, and approaching. He could not smell anything, the tent obscuring that sense, but Zephyr knew it was not friendly. It was stalking. Hunting.

He pulled away from Gawain carefully, and the knight awakened quickly, sitting up as Zephyr lifted away his wing. Gawain opened his mouth to speak, but he noticed the quiet almost immediately and got to his feet with fluid grace, dragging on his clothing. Zephyr crept for the flap of the tent and nudged it open with his snout, sucking in a deep breath.

Humans. Unwashed, stinking of wet furs, steel, and old blood. Zephyr growled softly, tail swishing, claws digging into the tent flooring.

Gawain tugged on his chain mail shirt and belted it fast, his sword and dagger put in place on his hips. The knight pulled on his boots, the ties left half undone before he went to the bed so he could pull them back on faster. He raced to Zephyr and knelt beside his head, a hand coming to move aside the flap so he could see out into the night. He leaned into Zephyr, and his whisper was softer than a night breeze, "What is it?"

"Ambush," Zephyr hissed back. "Dangerous humans."

Gawain's face went to stone, eyes cold, jaw set to steel. He threw open the tent flap and yelled as he drew his sword. "Ambush! Knights to arms!"

Shouts came from the tents in the camp, and Avril burst from the tent beside them just as Gawain and Zephyr left their own. The fire was still burning but low, and it was ominously dark where the other fire should have been burning by the horses.

Shouts came from everywhere and chaos erupted as knights and ambushers clashed. A shadow came out from the darkness alongside the rear of the tent, forming into a man with a sword raised high, screaming. The attacker aimed for Gawain's back, and Zephyr twisted around and leapt past Gawain, crashing into the man. Jaws latched onto the attacker's shoulder and neck and Zephyr bit down hard, flesh and bone rending under the pressure. A strangled gurgle bubbled up as blood ran from the human's mouth, and he died as Zephyr spit him out with a snarl. He spun, wings lifted, tail thrashing, and sprinted after Gawain as the knight ran into the fray.

Gawain fought with a savage efficiency, sword flashing in the low light from the fire. Two humans were dead before Zephyr caught up with the knight. Two more men came from the darkness, and they were clothed in rough wool and furs. The blades they raised to attack were shiny and smelled freshly of a forge, and the oddity was set aside as they closed in on Gawain. Zephyr dragged in a deep breath, dropped his jaw, and pushed out a burst of flame that caught the man on the left, quickly engulfing him. A scream cut short shattered the night, and the man fell, his burning flesh illuminating the shadows, light bouncing off the tents and the running figures of humans. Gawain took out the other attacker who had stumbled to a shocked halt as his fellow attacker burned.

Light exploded with a resounding boom overhead, a million tiny white stars eradicating the night as they spread out in a wave several dragon lengths above. The entire clearing, the section of road along the camp, and part of the woods were illuminated, brighter than midsummer day. Zephyr shook his head as his eyes adjusted, and the men attacking from the woods stood out in stark relief in their rough-spun gear and furs. Tristan stood backlit by a small army of white stars, magical fire burning the air around him, hands reaching out and shooting blasts of energy, knocking down the men charging at him. The mage spun gracefully, hands flowing, spinning out magic and spells with chilling efficiency, sending those foolish enough to attack him tumbling a dozen feet across the field head over ass. None of them got up.

Gawain clashed with another ruffian, sword slicing across the man's ribs in a spray of blood, making short work of his opponent. Zephyr ducked around Gawain and his kill, slamming into another man armed with an axe. The blade bounced off the spikes on his neck, and Zephyr bit down hard on the human's skull, crunching bone and flesh. A hard twitch and the human died, and he dropped the body, spitting out hair with a growl.

Zephyr shadowed Gawain as they moved through the camp, dispatching the men attacking as they went. Gawain fought with a fierceness that wouldn't be out of place in a dragon, his sword catching the light from the stars above, deadly as fang and claw. No one who went against him stood a chance.

Gawain pulled his sword from the latest man to engage with him, and Zephyr hissed and prowled in a circle around his knight, looking for more enemies that threatened them. No one moved in the shadows, and the magical starlight showed the dark silhouettes of bodies strewn through the field and throughout the camp. Gawain spun back for the center of the camp with Zephyr on his heels.

Tristan was there beside the remains of the central fire, the embers kicked into the damp grass and extinguished, smoke curling into the air. He was bent over one of the squires, the male named Jon, who was bleeding from a gaping wound in his shoulder. The flesh lay split from collarbone to elbow, and blood flowed in a thick wave from the injury, the squire white from blood loss and breathing in desperate gasps.

Gawain's face went tight, and his eyes were haunted, but he didn't interrupt, instead running for Avril and Bedivere who were leaning on each other, swords hanging limply in their grasps. "Find our people," Gawain ordered. "I want an accounting of everyone."

The knights nodded and tore off in opposite directions, and Gawain gestured for Zephyr to stay by the fire. "Stay and guard Tristan while he works, please." Zephyr nodded and crouched down on the other side of the cold fire. Gawain gathered up Axton and Evern who came out from the edge of camp and they went to find the rest of their people.

"I'm going to die," Jon gasped out, terrified. He was deathly pale, skin clammy. Magic roiled in the air above the wound, and Tristan shook his head as he worked, hands hovering over the horrible injury.

"No, I won't let you," Tristan retorted, determined. His magic slowed the blood flow, and Zephyr marveled that the squire was still alive. He must have been injured right next to the mage for him to even be alive this long. White light glimmered over the flesh where it was sliced open, and Zephyr watched as the muscles and veins and the other bits of the human slowly knit back together. "Dammit, I need more hands." Tristan quickly looked up, but no one was nearby, and he swore under his breath. Jon passed out, head lolling back, but he wasn't dead since Zephyr could still hear his heart beating. It didn't sound right, and he knew the human was close to dying.

"I get help?" Zephyr asked, ready to bolt for another human.

"Yes! Dammit!" Tristan swore again, hands shaking. "I need someone to hold the flesh together so I can bind it. It's taking too long this way."

Zephyr had finger-like claws on his front paws, but they were too big to help. Tristan poured more magic into the wound, shaking as he worked. The squire was a slim young man, muscled from work with hands that should have looked delicate but were calloused from use. He was not awake to assist in his own healing, and Zephyr looked up again, spotting a cluster of injured people being tended to a few tents away. Everyone was busy, and from what he could hear, there was another serious injury or two being tended to as well.

He needed hands. Zephyr's magic was replenished, and while he'd never transformed into another creature like a human, hands were needed. Tristan was frantic, and Zephyr wanted to help. The mage cared deeply for the squire, and the pain and frustration radiating off the older man stirred Zephyr into trying.

He called to his magic and pushed at his form from within, asking it to bend to the task he required.

Pain radiated out from his bones, and his scales split with a snap and hiss of embers in a fire. He did not know the shape he needed, so he reached out and touched the hand of the squire where his uninjured arm lay out flung in the grass. He could not copy another creature exactly, but his magic learned the shape of a human from the touch as he roused it. He pushed harder, his vision of the camp and the night blurring.

His vision returned, and it was odd—he could see more in

front of him than he normally could, and his peripheral vision was reduced, though the colors were more vivid. The air was colder, the grass wet beneath him, and he shivered, but he crawled across the grass on his newly formed hands and knees and shakily reached out to grab the edges of the wound, pushing it together as Tristan gasped with effort. Blood made his new fingers slippery, but he'd not made the transformation before so he still had some small scales on his hands and fingers, helping him keep his grip.

Tristan did not look up from his task, muttering as he went, and Zephyr moved his grip ahead of the spellwork, able to see it as the mage reknit torn flesh and skin. He pushed and tugged the raw flesh into place as Tristan worked, and the wound knit itself back together behind his fingers, moving faster now that a pair of hands was helping. Soon the massive injury was closed, and Zephyr fell back on his bare ass, covered in blood and shivering. Tristan fell back on his heels and searched for a pulse on the squire's neck, exclaiming in relief when he found it.

"Thank you—," Tristan lifted his head, and his words cut off mid-sentence as the mage looked at him. Zephyr tilted his head and held up his hands, flexing the fingers and wrists. The blood was rapidly cooling and sticky as it dried.

His skin was no longer scale and hide, though lines of orange and black scales decorated his fingers and hands in random patterns, smooth on the surface and not raised and separate like they had been in his true form. Human limbs now were covered in smooth skin, a light golden color with sparse thin hairs on his arms and legs. He looked down, and his human legs were bent beneath him, knees turning the opposite way his legs went as a dragon, and the random lines of scale in orange and black flowed down his sides along his ribs and hips. Zephyr stared curiously at his groin, tilting his head to the side as he examined the weird appendage between his legs. What fascinated him the most though were his legs, and he kicked them out from underneath himself and wiggled his toes. The wind chilled his back and shoulders, and he twitched as he realized he didn't have wings in his human body.

Zephyr squeaked in surprise then rolled onto his side and looked behind himself, but his tail was gone too. How very odd, though he shouldn't be surprised as humans didn't have tails or wings. He felt off balance for a moment but reasoned he could have them back if he returned to his true form.

"Tristan," Gawain returned to the center of the camp, looking down at the mage and the still breathing Jon. "Will he be all right?"

Tristan snapped out of his shock and shook his head before answering Gawain. "He should be. I got some help in time." Tristan gestured to Zephyr, who was sprawled out on the damp grass.

He was growing cold in his human form, yet he wasn't in a rush to change back. Being a human was different, even if he was cold and wet. Zephyr sniffed as he realized he'd used up a great deal of his magic, and he would need to wait for it to recharge before he switched back. His first transformation in years all but wiped him out.

Gawain looked down at him in mounting confusion.

"My Gawain," Zephyr said, and he surprised himself with how different his voice sounded. Gone were the hisses, and his voice was lighter, and the words felt different in his human mouth. He licked at his blunt teeth, marveling at the differences.

9

Gawain had never been so shocked in his life, and he had seen some truly terrible and awe-inspiring things. Yet nothing in his life had ever prepared him for the heart-shot realization of just who it was he was looking at in the grass at his feet.

The young human male was beautiful and strange, and it was his eyes that solidified his identity for Gawain. Zephyr's ember eyes glowed back up at him, still split like a cat's, the color the same, though now smaller and staring back at him from a human face. Orange, red and black scales danced in a thin line down the side of his heart-shaped face and cherubic hair tumbled into red and black curls that fell to his shoulders. The scales went in a line down the sides of his neck, down his shoulders to his sides, and branched out down his arms in random spots to his fingers. The same happened on his legs, the sleek, toned muscles clearly defined under smooth and soft-looking skin, unmarked by scars or time. Dainty feet and tiny perfect toes with black toenails completed the transformation, and Zephyr purred at him from the ground, his sweet face full of satisfied happiness.

"My Gawain!" His voice was light and gentle, and it made Gawain snap out of his shock. Zephyr was somehow human, though not entirely, and he was naked in the cold damp air after they'd just survived an ambush. Priorities shifted and Gawain sheathed his sword then tugged his tunic up and over his head and knelt by Zephyr. Heart hammering under his ribs, Gawain looked over the blood on Zephyr's hands and arms, though there were no injuries that Gawain could see. Zephyr was even more vulnerable in this form without the protection of his scales and claws and fire. He had to be kept safe.

Gawain tugged the tunic down over Zephyr's head. Zephyr was swamped by the garment, the tunic easily three times too large, and he was adorable when his head popped through the collar and his curls tumbled about his shoulders.

"Gawain!" He spun, hand on his sword hilt, and Avril stumbled to a halt, staring down in shock at Zephyr. She shook her head, forgoing asking questions, and spoke. "I need Tristan. Is Jon..."

"He's alive," Tristan said as he got slowly to his feet. "Someone get him into a tent and under some blankets. I'm coming." He followed Avril, both hurrying back toward where a few others were injured. Gawain was of no use in magical healing, so he'd come for Tristan, terrified he would find the squire dead, but a miracle had occurred, and the young man lived. Two miracles, really, and he looked down at Zephyr who was playing with the hem of the tunic, his fingers covered in dried blood.

He knelt beside Jon and scooped the squire into his arms as gently as he could. He took him into the nearest tent and laid him down on a pallet. He tucked the squire under a thick wool blanket, checking for a pulse. Weak, but steady. He backed out of the tent then went to Zephyr, the young dragon—man—who was staring at his feet while he wiggled his toes.

Gawain crouched down beside Zephyr, who smiled wide, revealing two sharp fangs where his human cuspid teeth should be. Two smaller fangs poked up from his lower jaw, daintier than the top pair, blending in with the more human teeth around them. His lips were pink and plump and shiny, and Gawain firmly told his body to ignore the charms of the hapless dragon in human form. Zephyr might be human-shaped, but he was still a dragon and surely had no idea he had transformed into a very attractive young man.

"My Gawain, look! Toes!" Zephyr pointed at his feet, happily examining the digits as he wiggled them again. "Aren't they marvelous?"

"They are lovely," Gawain murmured with a soft smile. He grunted when Zephyr threw himself forward and wrapped slim arms around his neck.

"Oh! A hug! You're bigger than me now! Arms are wonderful!" Zephyr exclaimed again, squirming in Gawain's arms until he was seated across the knight's lap with his face pressed to Gawain's shoulder, sniffing and rubbing his face into the bare skin along Gawain's neck. "You feel so different now, but the same. It's strange."

A pert ass rubbed over his groin, and Gawain gasped, arms reflexively closing about Zephyr and holding him still, safe in his embrace. "Zephyr, I need to secure the camp and make sure all my people are safe and getting help if they're injured," Gawain stood, Zephyr weighing next to nothing, a far change from the other day when he all but squished Gawain in the nest of pillows. "You are perfect just as you are, but can you change back? I'm afraid to leave you alone while I see to things."

Zephyr pulled back, a tiny frown on his kissable lips. His nose scrunched up, eyes narrowing, and then he shook his head and relaxed. "I used all of my magic giving myself hands. Once it comes back I can."

He understood only the barest amount, but he figured it wasn't all that different than Tristan exhausting his magic after using it for extended periods of time. Tristan usually needed a day to replenish himself and some sleep and good food. "All right, I'm putting you in the tent with Jon. Keep an eye on him and call out if he stops breathing or looks to be getting worse. Can you do that for me?"

Zephyr nodded eagerly, and Gawain carried him over to the tent and ducked within. He set Zephyr beside the unconscious squire, who still breathed, though he appeared pale and wan. Zephyr sat beside the other young man and tucked the blankets in around him, hovering protectively. Gawain smiled and pulled his dagger from his belt and held it hilt first to Zephyr. The young dragon eyed it curiously and took it with one slim and graceful hand, delicate fingers wrapping around the steel and leather hilt. "If a stranger comes in here, scream for help. Use this to defend yourself. I will be back for you as fast as I can."

"Yes, Gawain," Zephyr said softly, eyes wide and trusting and just as pretty in a human face as they had been in his dragon form.

Gawain gave him a reassuring smile then left the tent, closing the flap behind him. He went about the business of securing the campsite and making an accounting of his people and the enemy. Why they were attacked was something he needed to answer as well, whether unhappy coincidence or pertaining to their mission to the hills around Morvain remained to be determined, and he couldn't delay learning the truth any longer.

He also had to tell his people that their dragon had done something amazing and unexpected, and the strange young man in their midst wasn't one of the men who ambushed them in the night.

Zephyr kept the heavy dagger on the pillow beside his hand, the one closest to the tent entrance, and listened to the squire breathing as he rested. Nothing but the young man's head was visible, and Zephyr made sure he was warm.

The garment he wore was thick and padded and smelled of Gawain, a delicious scent that made him snuggle down into the fabric and breath in deeply. His sense of smell was weaker, but the scent of his knight was imbedded in the piece of clothing, and he was very pleased to be covered in it. It was warm, and he was happy for it, as he could feel the temperature in a way he hadn't before. His human feet were cold, and he pulled them in and hugged himself as he tried to hold off the damp chill.

The humans were busy and the light from the mage's stars cast a white glow over the top of the tent, shadows of people running back and forth as they dealt with the aftermath of the attack. Humans were violent, and Zephyr wondered what the goal was for the attackers. Maybe they wanted the supplies the knights had? They did not want for food, had many weapons, and the armor and chainmail the knights traveled with would offer protection more than the leathers and furs worn by the marauders.

Zephyr sighed and rested his head on his knees, reaching out with one hand every few minutes to touch the squire's neck, finding the pulse point and reassuring himself that the young human was alive. His senses were a bit different than they would be in his true form, and while he could hear the beat of the human's heart, the noise from outside the tent was hard to sift through and ignore.

He lost track of time, and when Gawain entered the tent, he jumped. Gawain gave him a soft smile and knelt by his side. "It's just me. How are you both doing?"

Zephyr leaned forward, and Gawain caught him close. Zephyr snuggled into the knight's muscled chest, breathing in deeply before speaking. "The squire lives. Been asleep since he was healed. I am cold."

Tristan entered the tent, and he helped Felix in as well, the knight limping on one leg, the other bandaged around the thigh, and his clothing covered in blood. "Gawain, take Zephyr back to your tent. I need the room for Jon and Felix." Avril stood visible just outside the tent entrance, one hand on her sword, alert as she searched the area, even though the danger seemed to be past.

Gawain picked up his dagger and flipped it around, sheathing it without looking, then stood with Zephyr in his arms. He headed out of the tent. Avril went in as they left, and the tent flap closed behind her.

The campfire had been relit, and the stars Tristan cast for light were still present, though not as many. A few hung just above the tents and provided enough light to illuminate anyone approaching from outside the camp. The mage was powerful to be able to cast the stars, fight with magic, then heal grievous wounds during and after a battle. He was glad the mage was a friend and not an enemy.

The other knights were gathered in a cluster as they spoke in low tones, and many of them looked no worse for wear despite the ambush. A couple had scrapes, and they could all use baths to clean off the blood splattered on their clothing and gear. Gawain paused and shifted his grip on him. Zephyr kept his arms firmly around Gawain's neck; the knight's arms were under his knees and behind his back, holding him securely. Gawain was warm, and Zephyr snuggled, trying to absorb some of the heat.

"Who was on watch when we were ambushed?" Gawain asked. Evern and Axton stepped forward. Neither knight was injured, though they were covered in blood and dirty. "All right. Everyone is on watch, the two of you get some sleep. We'll talk in the morning."

The knights nodded, several of them casting inquisitive and astonished glances at Zephyr. He waved at them with one hand, and Axton, shocked, waved back. Zephyr snuggled back into Gawain's embrace, who hugged him tightly. "I'll explain things better in the morning."

Gawain carried Zephyr into his tent and put him down on the nest of pillows. Zephyr wiggled and squirmed until he found a comfortable position, blinking up at Gawain sleepily. Zephyr wore the thick leather garment Gawain had given him earlier, and Gawain murmured something about how it would be uncomfortable to sleep in. His knight grabbed an under-tunic from the pile of clothing he wore the day before and tugged off the gambeson, pulling the undertunic over Zephyr's head. He was enjoying the tender touches and care.

Gawain shook his head and went to the rear of the tent where a small chest that held his clothing had a basin and pitcher of water resting on top with some towels. Gawain washed briefly in the mornings before they broke camp, so the water was fresh and clean. Gawain wet a cloth and came back to the pillow nest.

He cleaned Zephyr's hands, one finger at a time, rubbing and wiping away the dried blood from his skin. The knight paused in his ministrations to occasionally run a finger over the red, orange, and black scales that ran in random patterns over his knuckles and the back of his hands. He didn't say anything, just tenderly cleaned Zephyr until the towel was stained red and the blood was gone.

"When we get back to the capital, I can run you a real bath," Gawain murmured, before sitting back and tossing the dirty cloth in the back corner. He chuckled softly. "You might be a dragon again by then, though. I'm sure you can clean yourself however you need to, but blood on skin is messy and things turn gross fairly quickly if not washed off sooner rather than later."

"I've never had a bath," Zephyr shared, putting his now clean hands around a pillow and pulling it to his belly. He yawned, and his jaw popped, then he relaxed into the nest. "Sleepy. Come sleep with me."

Gawain blinked at him, his face flushing, and his heart gave a hard thump before settling back into a normal, if faster, rhythm. "I'm going to let you relax and get some sleep. I have some dead bodies to sort out and other things." Gawain grabbed a blanket and pulled it over Zephyr, one big hand gently brushing his cheek before pulling away. "Sleep. I'll keep you safe."

10

Gawain rubbed a hand over his face and grimaced at the dirt and blood still on his fingers. The bodies of the men who attacked them in the middle of the night were lined up downwind of the camp, and Tristan would be burning their remains once he had sufficiently recovered from combat and healing injuries.

Bedivere and Evern finished searching the bodies and came back to Gawain where he stood not too far away, keeping a watchful eye on the tree line. Morning had come and gone, and the midday sun beat down on them. Thankfully the breeze was cool, and the shadows under the trees were colder than they had been the day before. The variations in the weather this early in spring were helping, though he had little doubt it would turn sweltering at some point soon. The bodies had yet to stink, and hopefully Tristan would take care of them before that happened.

"Sir," Bedivere held out a hand and Gawain took a few coins from his palm. "Coins from Medilan." Gawain cursed. The coins were indeed Medilan gold pieces, freshly stamped and unmarked by the exchange of hands. He looked over his shoulder, though nothing could be seen in the direction of their neighboring country except for the mountains between them. The same mountains that Zephyr flew over to escape the mage who held him captive.

"What are the odds that we get ambushed by bandits bearing coin from the country that Zephyr was fleeing?" Gawain mused aloud, and the grim expressions his knights bore told him they suspected the same. He swore under his breath then handed the coins back to Bedivere. "Anything else? Papers? Maybe jewelry or tattoos?"

"Some tattoos," Evern replied, scratching at a scrape on his neck he'd gotten sometime in the night. "Recognized some of the symbols and designs. Locals from the hills. Not really part of any townships—they tend to roam when the seasons change, but they haunt the hills between here and the border with Medilan."

"There's no passes in this area of the mountains," Gawain stated, though he doubted it for sure. Goat trails, maybe. But nothing a sizeable force could navigate without mass casualties and within the timeframe of summer when the highest reaches were tolerable for humans. Early spring down here in the lower elevations still meant the higher reaches were buried in snow and ice. A small party could make it through in summer, or a messenger looking to hire people to solve a problem, but not now. Magic could make it through, though. "A mage might be able to send a message through and faster than a human could navigate the few trails that exist this time of year."

"Think it's the mage who held Zephyr?" Bedivere asked, tossing a coin up and down absentmindedly as he frowned in thought. "They were carrying weapons meant for killing, but a few of them had lengths of rope and..." Bedivere paused and went to the nearby pile of gear taken from the corpses. Anything usable would be kept, the rest burned before they decamped. Bedivere rifled through the pile, then grabbed something and walked back over. He held out shackles, and Gawain took them, heart beating hard in his chest.

"These are too big for humans," Gawain stated, anger rising. He turned over the shackles, the metal surface shimmered oddly. His hands tingled, and he dropped the shackles quickly. "There's magic on them."

"They were after Zephyr," Evern came to the same conclusion Gawain had, and Gawain nodded, instinct telling him things weren't over.

"We need to get back to the capital. We're too exposed out here, too far from reinforcements. The mage may be coming himself to collect Zephyr since there's no way to get him back over the mountains safely—and he won't fly himself back there, that's for certain. A mage could handle getting across the mountains if he were powerful enough."

"We handled them easily enough," Bedivere jerked a thumb at the bodies. "We should be all right the deeper we get into Kentaine."

Gawain hummed, not agreeing entirely but not doubting their ability to handle another force coming for them. Mundane humans they could handle. "We almost lost Jon last night, and Felix is out—his leg needs more healing than Tristan can provide on the road in his current condition. Tristan can't fight if he's drained from healing."

"We need to get moving," Evern said. Tension rose as his knights shifted, growing more wary. Gawain nodded.

"Alert the servants they need to move supplies around to get a wagon equipped to handle our injured." Gawain kicked the shackles. "Get those to the smithy and have him destroy them before he breaks down his forge; it'll interrupt repairs of gear, but those are too dangerous to leave intact. I'll get Tristan to burn the bodies." Gawain held out his hand, and Bedivere handed over the coins. His sister was going to need tangible proof of Medilan's interference in Kentainian affairs. He doubted the Medilan royals were involved, but he couldn't be certain they were unaware one of their citizens was hunting a sentient being in another country.

Zephyr was under the protection of the Royal Family of Kentaine, but even more importantly, Zephyr was under his protection. Gawain wasn't going to let anything happen to Zephyr, no matter who came for him.

Hours later, the stench of burning flesh still hung in the air, despite the miles between them and their former camp. Zephyr's belly rumbled, but he didn't ask for more meat since they were traveling. He'd eyed the corpses before Gawain bundled him up into the wagon designated for the injured, the cloth covering hiding who was within. He didn't think the humans would appreciate him snacking on the other humans even if they were dead and enemies.

Zephyr peeked out the side of the wagon, seeing nothing but trees and a mounted knight riding alongside the wagon. The knights wore more armor, had weapons at hand, and they weren't to stop unless necessary. Gawain was grim and focused, his knights vigilant.

Jon slept in the wagon, and Felix was awake, the knight sitting upright, his sword near to hand. Blankets, pillows, and sleeping cushions kept them in relative comfort, though the rocking from the wagon's pace was making Zephyr queasy. It was an odd thing to experience motion sickness, and he leaned against the side of the wagon and moved aside the covering enough so he could get some fresh air.

He groaned when a wave of nausea hit him hard, and he swallowed back bile that threatened to escape.

"What's wrong?" Tristan asked from the front of the wagon, looking back at him from the opening right behind the bench seat.

"Wagons are evil," Zephyr growled. "Don't want to be back here."

"We have to keep you under cover," Tristan said, and it was the same refrain from that morning when Gawain ordered him to stay in the wagon out of sight. "We think you're being hunted."

Zephyr sighed and rolled his eyes, an experience he enjoyed in his human form. "They are looking for a dragon!"

"Yes, they are, so stay in there," Tristan retorted.

Zephyr shook his head, the long strands of his multi-colored hair flying around his shoulders. "Not a dragon now!" He was shaped like a human, and aside from the random scale lines, he was not what his pursuers were looking for anymore. His eyes and fangs were only noticeable up close, and as long as he stayed covered, no one would suspect anything.

Tristan blinked and shut his mouth. He chuckled then gave Zephyr a sharp smile. "All right, excellent point. Hold on." He dropped the covering back in place, and Zephyr heard him shout. The sound of the wagon over the gravel road obscured most of what they were saying. The clop of shod hooves grew loud, and Zephyr went to peek, but the wagon came to a halt before he could and the back opened. Gawain smiled at him from the back of his great warhorse, and he angled the beast so it stood sideways. The horse stamped a hoof and snorted loudly, but Gawain held him in check with ease.

"C'mon, we can't delay too long." Gawain held out his gloved hand, and Zephyr went to him without hesitation.

Gawain pulled him from the wagon and up in front of him in the saddle, though he rested across Gawain's muscular thighs more than the hard leather. The pommel of the saddle was far enough forward that it didn't dig into his hip, and Zephyr fell back on Gawain's strong chest with a happy sigh.

He was wearing borrowed linen leggings, thick wool stockings, and Gawain's tunic from that morning that he had refused to relinquish, so he wasn't as cold as he was before. His feet were too small, and no one had a pair of boots that fit him, but he didn't mind. Gawain was warm and he held Zephyr close, left hand holding the reins while his right wrapped around Zephyr with an iron grip. He made a low noise at his horse, and the beast tossed its head and rounded the wagon.

It was his first time on a horse, and he was thankful Gawain held him so tightly. He was as big as a horse in his true form, but as a human, he was small and easily broken, and the horse was tall and powerful. He clung to Gawain who rubbed a gloved hand along his side in reassurance. They moved along the side of the wagon, and Gawain paused just long enough for the mage to lean over on the bench seat and toss a brown cloak over Zephyr. "Pull the hood up if we encounter anyone on the road. Hide the scales."

Gawain helped Zephyr get under the cloak then, with that soft noise again, guided his mount back into formation on the road. The knights were arranged on all sides of the wagons, the one holding the injured men in the center of the convoy. Gawain resumed his position in front with Avril and Evern right behind him.

His knight smelled of leather and steel, his sword

sheathed in a scabbard attached to the saddle. A long dagger hung from his waist, and a chainmail shirt was under the surcoat—this one a black weave of silk and leather, the dragon in flight as black as night. The sunlight cutting through the patchy cloud cover above was absorbed by the metal and dark fabric, and Zephyr happily let it warm him, pressing his cheek to Gawain' s chest.

Gawain chuckled softly, and the arm holding him so securely tightened even more. Zephyr gave a low purr, not as deep as it would be in his true form, but hopefully it conveyed just how pleased he was with his current position.

The rocking motion of the horse was easy to adapt to as all he had to do was let Gawain move them both. Warmth from the sun and the man holding him lulled him into a light doze, and the sickness from being in the wagon passed almost immediately. He yawned wide, jaw clicking, then snuggled in as best he could, closing his eyes. One hand gripped the surcoat covering the chainmail, fingers tangling in the fabric.

"Sleep if you're tired," Gawain murmured, breath stirring the black and red curling strands of Zephyr's hair. It tickled, and he smiled. "I'll look after you."

He believed Gawain, the certainty settling into his heart along with the promise.

His magic was returning faster than before, growing in the depth of his reserves and recharging quicker than he expected. He could probably transform back into his true form, but the way Gawain's arms cradled him left him reluctant to make the change. Zephyr was curious about what else he could transform into, but he was enjoying being in a human shape too much to bother.

The retinue paused once for humans and horses alike to rest and eat, the humans going into the woods along the roads to relieve themselves in pairs under Gawain's directive. Gawain swung down from the saddle first then held out his arms to catch Zephyr as he slid down next. Gawain didn't even put him down, instead striding for the trees and brush, only stopping once they were just out of sight of the rest of the retinue. He was wondering how to use his human body to pass waste when Gawain solved the problem by opening his clothing and pulling out his member. Fascinated, Zephyr lifted the edge of his tunic and did the same, copying Gawain as the human aimed for the base of a tree and let go.

"Make sure to shake it off," Gawain said with a grin as he finished. "Try not to get any liquid on yourself or your clothing."

"Like this?" Zephyr finished, bladder empty, and copied Gawain's two brisk shakes. Gawain's organ was thick and long, and the scent of healthy male and sweat made him sniff, body tingling in interest. He wanted to get closer and see if the skin tasted as it smelled, delicious and musky. The length of flesh in his hands firmed and twitched as he watched Gawain tuck himself back inside his clothing, and Zephyr tugged, moaning softly.

"None of that now," Gawain chided, though his scent grew stronger, muskier, and his voice was rumbly and deep. "We need to get back on the road." Blue eyes locked on

Zephyr's fingers, and his member hardened even more, making him restless and aching.

"Feels good," Zephyr hissed out, and he gasped as a tug lit his nerves on fire, hips jerking. "Need something." He whined, frustrated, unsure of what he was doing but unable to stop. He looked up at Gawain, pleading, biting his lower lip and whimpering. "What's happening?"

Gawain flushed and sucked in a deep breath. "You got yourself too excited, and now you need to come. It's nothing bad; you'll be alright, I promise."

"Come?" Zephyr gasped out, fingers trailing over the fat head of the throbbing flesh standing eagerly from his groin.

"An orgasm," Gawain sounded strangled, and his breathing grew faster as his cheeks flushed.

"Oohh," Zephyr breathed out, understanding at last. His own scent helped him finally realize what was happening. His body wanted to mate and needed sexual release. Growing up, he saw many adult dragons sate their needs together or alone, but how humans did it was beyond him. "Help me? Please?"

"I can ...help you," Gawain sounded like he was in pain, but pheromones and heat rolled off him and flooded the air. "I can tell you how, or...I would have to touch you."

"Please, oh please," Zephyr gasped out, flesh aching and skin taut. "Please, touch me."

Gawain moved carefully, as if he were worried Zephyr would bolt. Zephyr whimpered in relief when Gawain pressed himself to Zephyr's back, arms circled around his waist. "Shh-hh," Gawain soothed him, and big, warm and callused hands took over. Steady, tight strokes from root to tip had Zephyr crying out, going to his tiptoes, arching back and leaning his weight on the reassuring and powerful frame of the man behind him. "My sweet dragon. Breathe. You're close, just let go."

He wanted to ask what Gawain meant, but fingers tugged

gently on the heavy sack of flesh swinging under the stiff member, and Zephyr gave in to an explosion of white-hot need and arousal. White, thick fluid spurted from the head and landed in the leaves at their feet. Another tightening of muscles, and Zephyr cried out, more fluid shooting out. The experience was slightly alarming, but with Gawain holding him, the fear never grew and faded away completely as his body relaxed, mind and muscles swamped with a calming afterglow that left him wanting to sleep.

Gawain gently tucked him back under the tunic then turned him around. Zephyr hugged him as best he could despite wanting to curl up and sleep, and he breathed in the scent of human sex and the heat rolling off Gawain. He leaned in and felt a throbbing hardness pressed against this belly. It took him a moment, then he realized it was Gawain's member, throbbing under his clothes. He wiggled, trying to get closer, wanting to touch it as Gawain had touched him.

"Careful," Gawain gasped. Zephyr tipped his head back and met Gawain's heated gaze.

"You're hard too. Should I help you?" He reached down, but Gawain caught his wrist in an iron grip.

Gawain sighed, a rueful smile on his lips. "I'll be alright. We need to get going." He paused, then gently lifted Zephyr's hand and kissed the inside of his wrist, easing his grip. "Are you okay with what we just did?"

Zephyr tilted his head to the side, confused. "I felt good, and you helped. I want to feel good together. With my Gawain."

"We can talk about that," Gawain murmured with a grin. "But right now, we have to get back on the road."

Back in the saddle with the day gone and evening waning towards night, Zephyr sat up from a doze he'd spent happily against Gawain. The surface of the road sang out under hooves, the dirt and gravel giving way to stone and hard-packed white gravel. Small bridges covered meandering streams that dotted the green fields, and the trees thinned out, becoming copses between fenced pastures. Cattle grazed in the distance on farms interspersed throughout the countryside. The hills were still rolling downward from the mountains that were growing smaller behind them as they traveled in a general southwesterly direction. In the distance, smoke rose from many chimneys, and lamplight glowed as twilight darkened.

"Sora," Gawain called over his shoulder. The scout prodded her mount forward from the middle of the convoy to the front to match pace with Gawain's warhorse. The scout peered at Zephyr, smugly content on Gawain's lap, and she chuckled.

"Sir Gawain?"

"Ride ahead to the village, see if the inn has room for us all. Contact the local healer and have them meet us at the village green or market square if the inn is full, or at the inn if we're staying the night there."

"Yes, Sir." Sora clicked at her mount, and the horse trotted ahead of the group a distance before she gave it its head and it broke into a long lope. The pounding of hooves gradually diminished as she faded from view.

"We're stopping for the night?" Bedivere asked from where he rode on Gawain's right.

"I don't want to push Jon or Felix more than we have to," Gawain explained. "Tristan needs the rest as well. We push on only if the inn can't take us."

"I'll let Tristan know," Avril said, reining in her mount so it dropped back toward the wagons.

"An inn?" Zephyr looked up at Gawain, curious. He could understand from context it was a place to stay temporarily but that was it.

"Aye," Gawain replied, and his cheeks flushed again, blue

eyes heated. "A bed, a hot meal, and we can push harder tomorrow once we're rested."

"A bed?" Zephyr had never seen a bed. As a dragon, he made a nest of available comfy materials, or slept on the earth. Stone was great to sleep on, especially in the evening after the rock absorbed heat from the sun all day. "I've never slept in a bed."

"As a dragon, I don't see why you would, unless it was very large." Gawain smiled down at him. "But since you're...now human-sized, a bed is a good idea... Far superior to a pillow nest."

Zephyr frowned. "I like your pillow nest."

"I like it too." His knight smiled down at him. "But a man needs a bed to get a decent night's sleep. Beds are good for other things, as well."

"Other things?"

Gawain flushed again. "I'll explain if we're stopping for the night."

Sleeping together with Gawain in his human form appealed, and he hoped they were stopping for the night.

11

Mel and Ari dipped their heads as they left, carrying Gawain's leathers and chainmail shirt with them. The gear would be returned in the morning, cleaned and any repairs needed made before breakfast. His sword and long dagger were wrapped up in his belt, leaning against the bed within easy reach if he needed them in the night.

Gawain shut the door of the room under the eaves, the pinnacle of the roof high enough he could stretch out and relax. Zephyr darted about the room, the borrowed leggings removed, barefoot and wearing the same tunic he'd put on the young dragon the other day. They'd thankfully get a chance to bathe and swap out clothing before getting back on the road for the capital.

Zephyr eyed the copper tub curiously, the water steaming. The inn servants had filled it two thirds of the way, carrying the water up in buckets one by one. The buckets were spelled to keep the water warm, a small luxury in the tiny town, but the town boasted a healer with magic, so buying spells for the inn was possible if it had enough income. Hosting a royal and his retinue meant more tiny hospitality spells could be bought and maintained. Fingers trailing over the surface, Zephyr made a small inquisitive noise in his throat, head tilting. He was shaped like a human, but his mannerisms were still dragon. He walked quickly, stopped and started, and every motion was efficient and self-aware. Sometimes his shoulders twitched, as if he were trying to move his wings, and his body was confused by their absence.

"Traveling in human form has hopefully thrown off any pursuers." Gawain tugged his undertunic up and over his head, throwing it over the back of one of the two chairs in the room. "If you were in your dragon form, getting you to the capital would be difficult."

"Why?" Zephyr asked, and he saw Gawain undressing and whipped off the borrowed tunic with a swirl of fabric, letting it drop to the floor. He was gloriously naked, and the lines of scales glittered in the lamplight.

"Getting a dragon past the townspeople and still making good time is hard enough in theory, but in practice, it wouldn't be safe. A dragon hasn't been seen in this country in over a hundred years, and most of the tales people know are about vicious predators with unstoppable magic and a tendency to eat knights of the realm." Gawain couldn't help but look over Zephyr's naked form, the young dragon unbothered by his nudity and too busy playing with the bath water to notice, or perhaps care, that Gawain could not look away. "We'd have startled and potentially frightened townspeople all the way to the palace, and I don't want violence to erupt like it did in Morvain."

Zephyr hummed and splashed a bit, water dripping to the sheepskin rug placed under the tub to catch spills. It too bore a spell to prevent the water from leaking through the floorboards to the room below, and it was an old spell, long-maintained, likely only brought out on rare occasions when the inn had a distinguished guest. Gawain shook his head. "That's for bathing, little dragon, not playing. Get in without spilling too much water and wash off."

Excitement bloomed on Zephyr's face, and the young dragon eagerly slid into the tub, a small wave of water sloshing over the edge before settling back into the tub. The water was still too hot for Gawain, but Zephyr merely smiled contentedly and stretched out before leaning back on the side of the tub. He was small enough the water came up to just below his shoulders, and his legs weren't as cramped as Gawain's would be when it was his turn to bathe.

Gawain went to the table and sat in one of the chairs, the tub a foot or so away where it had been placed in front of the fireplace. He grabbed a bar of soap from his sidebag on the table and handed it to Zephyr. It was a scrubbing soap made from powdered pumice stone and mutton tallow mixed with lavender. Zephyr sniffed it, and before he could say anything, licked the bar. Zephyr's expression of disgust made him laugh aloud. "No, love. Scrub your skin with the soap, don't eat it." He tossed a cleaning rag in the tub as well. "Get that sudsy and start washing."

"Sudsy?" Zephyr appeared confused, but he figured it out before Gawain could show him. Wash cloth in one hand and soap in the other, Zephyr wasted no time in cleaning his body. His happy murmurs as he went about it made Gawain chuckle. He stopped though and blinked at Gawain in concern. "Is Gawain going to wash?"

"I will, once you're done." His answer seemed to satisfy Zephyr as he went back to cleaning himself, humming under his breath. He was certainly appreciating his first bath. Gawain was appreciating it too, though for a different reason, and that made a pang of guilt crash into the low burn of lust in his blood. "If I made you uncomfortable earlier in the woods, I am sorry."

"What do you mean?" Zephyr was bendy, one leg pulled up so he could clean his feet. Suds bubbled up around the tub.

"I touched you, in a sexual way. You're under my protection."

"Sex is what adults do when they want each other. Dragons have sex when they want it," Zephyr said, eyes calm, curiosity in his tone. "Do humans not have sex when they want it?"

Gawain shifted in his seat, a bit uncomfortable with the topic but refusing to hold his tongue. "Humans should only have sex when both are adults and can consent. Sex without consent is wrong. Taking advantage of someone who is too young to give consent or doesn't understand what's happening in general is wrong, too."

Zephyr paused in washing, putting down his foot and tilting his head. His hair, a very unusual combination of black and red strands, slid off his shoulder and the ends dipped into the water. "I am grown. Not grown for long, and I am smaller than I should be, but I am grown. Dragons have sex when they are grown, and only then, and they mate when there are shared needs. I learned this young, fresh from my egg."

"Really?" That was very young. Dragons and humans were different in that regard for certain.

Zephyr nodded. "I learned by watching the dragons around me. We learn by watching and listening and playing. I was too young for mating when I was taken with my brood-mother, but once I had my adult molting, I was grown, and could do such things if I wanted. Other dragons would know I was grown by my scales, and if they wanted to mate, would display for me. If I wanted to mate, I would do the same in return."

Interesting. Birds displayed for potential mates, dancing

and preening and doing other things to impress. "So you haven't mated?"

"Not before my knight," Zephyr went back to washing. "Was held captive with my broodmother. Blood too close for mating. She taught me about mating before she died, but I never had a chance to try as a grown dragon."

A virgin then, but not ignorant. Gawain let go of his shadowy guilt as best he could. Zephyr might not know about human sex, but he understood something about sex in the abstract. Consent seemed to be the common thread between their species.

"She was your mother?" He figured as much, but how dragons bred was a bit of a mystery. Eggs for sure, but how they traced their lineage was something the chronicles never mentioned.

"She was the one who laid my egg."

"What was her name?" Gawain flinched, reining in his curiosity. "I'm sorry, I know she died."

"Broodmother was Araceli."

"A lovely name," Gawain replied. "I am sorry for your loss."

"Freed when dead." Zephyr frowned, sadness in his eyes, before sighing and shaking his head, hair flopping down his forehead. Zephyr tugged at the ends, fascinated. "My Gawain, wash hair?"

"Just duck under the water and wet your hair," Gawain offered, and Zephyr went under before he finished explaining. The dragon popped back up almost immediately, sputtering and wiping at his eyes.

Chuckling, Gawain grabbed a ewer set on the hearth and dipped it in the tub. "Close your eyes and hold your breath." Zephyr obeyed and Gawain poured the water over his head, slicking back the strands away from Zephyr's face. "Hold on, let me wash your hair."

He grabbed the bar of soap that floated in the water, lathered up his hands and worked the soap into Zephyr's hair. The red strands grew more brilliant in the water, glittering, and the black strands darkened even more, shiny as gem-cut obsidian. Zephyr purred as he massaged the scalp, carding his fingers through the shoulder-length strands to make sure there were no knots. Zephyr needed a comb if he was going to be human for longer periods of time.

"Let me rinse, keep your eyes closed."

Zephyr hummed agreeably, and Gawain carefully poured the water over his head, working the hair to make sure it rinsed clean. He set the ewer aside and then reached for a towel from the short stack on the hearth.

He wiped Zephyr's face, then rubbed his hair gently, squeezing to catch the water. "Stand up carefully and take the towel."

Zephyr put his hands on the rim and got to his feet, water cascading down his lithe form, and Gawain politely looked away, holding the towel up and out. Zephyr blinked at him, obviously confused, and Gawain sighed ruefully and wrapped the towel around Zephyr under his arms. It covered him from shoulder to mid-thigh, and Gawain grabbed another towel then held out his hand. "Step out, then dry yourself off."

Zephyr took his hand and climbed out, water dripping on the rug.

Zephyr was enthusiastic with the towel, rubbing himself everywhere with it. Gawain quickly disrobed, and Zephyr paused in his mad flurry of toweling to stare at Gawain's nude body as he stepped into the still warm water. He made quick work of washing and untied his hair from the tail tied at the nape of his neck. Gawain soaped and rinsed his hair just as quickly, not wanting to sit in cold water.

"My Gawain?"

Gawain squeezed water from his hair then threw it over one shoulder. "Yes?"

"Will I need to be a human for a long time?"

Gawain paused for a moment, getting to his feet. Zephyr was naked again, the towels in his lap, his beautiful hair in a riot of curls and waves from toweling it dry. His expression was pensive, and he nibbled on a plump lower lip while he looked at Gawain anxiously.

He stood and stepped from the tub, grabbing the last towel from the hearth and drying himself quickly. He tossed it aside and went to his sidebags, tugging out a pair of knee-length braies and pulling them on. Zephyr watched him intently, eyes taking in every muscle, ridge, and silver scar on his skin.

Gawain pulled out a clean tunic, this one meant for wearing about camp or lounging in his suite at home in the palace, and went to where Zephyr sat, holding it out. Zephyr reached for it, fingers curling into the fabric, and Gawain held on for a moment, just long enough for Zephyr to meet his gaze. "You are easier to hide in your human form. Once we get you safely to the palace, you can return to your natural state and never be a man again if that's what you want. If we made it seem like you couldn't be a dragon again, I am sorry." Gawain let go of the tunic, and Zephyr pulled it to his chest, playing with the folds.

Zephyr said nothing, and Gawain looked around the room. It was the second largest the inn had available, the largest going to the injured and Tristan and Avril, who were caring for Jon and Felix. The town healer came and went, saying rest would be the best treatment after a session of working on Felix's leg. The room Gawain got for himself became Zephyr's as well, the dragon declaring loudly in the common room when they entered the inn that he couldn't wait to sleep with Gawain in a bed instead of a nest. The innkeeper had gawked, Tristan laughed, and Gawain held back a smile at the guileless anticipation on his face.

Luckily, his hair hid the scales along the sides of his face and down his neck, and the common room was dark enough in the lamplight that the slit pupils weren't easily seen. Gawain had some worry when the reflective quality of Zephyr's eyes caught the lamplight, but the innkeeper had been busy gathering help to get them settled upstairs.

Zephyr stood and put the tunic on the table, moving slowly. Gawain worried that Zephyr was insulted or hurt, maybe both, that their traveling was made easier by asking him to keep his human form. "The room is small, but if you're careful, you can transform back into a dragon for the night. You'd need to transform back into this form to get out, since the door and windows are too small. If you want to keep to your natural form, I'll make it work. I can borrow some guardsmen from the town watch to act as crowd control as we get closer to the capital."

Lips pursed as his jaw tensed, Zephyr appeared to be pondering something. He looked at the bed, and Gawain couldn't help his body's reaction. He found Zephyr's human form attractive, but he refused to make Zephyr hold a form that wasn't natural to him just so Gawain could enjoy looking at him. He said nothing, refusing to influence the dragon's decision.

Zephyr walked naked to the bed and crawled onto it with low, slinking movements. He fussed with the blankets, but then figured out how to pull them down and slid under them. Slitted eyes caught the candlelight, reflecting like colored mirrors, then Zephyr smiled, revealing his fangs. "If I return to my true form, I cannot sleep with you, skin to skin. My magic will be drained for a day or more, and I would have to wait." Zephyr leaned toward Gawain, a hand with a shimmer of scales over the back of it sliding over the cotton sheets. "Nest is warm. Come sleep."

Gawain ran a hand through his still damp hair, stalling for time. "Skin to skin?" Rough, and deeper than he intended, the words rumbled out from him, and a fine shiver went over the slim form in the bed, beckoning to him.

"My Gawain," Zephyr purred, and turned his hand over, curling his fingers in a come-hither gesture that lit a fire in Gawain's blood.

Gawain was moving before he gave thought to the action. A quick tug and his sleep pants fell to the floor, and he was at the bed and slipping under the bedclothes a heartbeat later. Slim but muscled limbs tangled with his, and a luscious smile welcomed him closer. Zephyr fit in his arms as if born for it, and Gawain groaned when silky smooth and hot skin met his hardening cock. He rolled them until he was hovering over Zephyr, whose red and black hair was spread over a pillow with vibrant scales shimmering in the shadows along his hairline. Zephyr panted in arousal, his cock growing against Gawain's thigh, eyes wide, mouth parted as a pink tongue wet his lower lip.

"My Gawain," Zephyr whispered, arching up into him.

"Yes?" Gawain asked, just as quietly, tension riding his muscles.

"Show me how humans mate." Zephyr's request hit like a small punch to the belly, and he groaned, his restraint evaporating in a flash. Such a sweetly innocent and demanding little dragon.

Gawain lowered his head until they were sharing breaths. Ember eyes met his gaze, and he spoke softly but clearly. "If you don't like anything I do, you can tell me to stop, and I will stop. If you want to stop completely and just go to sleep, you can say that anytime you want, and I will stop."

"Yes, my Gawain," Zephyr purred. "I will do the same for

you." And with that sweet promise, his wet pink tongue flicked out and licked along Gawain's lips.

Thinking Zephyr wasn't intending a kiss but not one to pass up a chance to show the dragon how it was done Gawain took Zephyr's mouth in an open-mouthed kiss. Fingers dug into his hair and gripped, but instead of pushing him away, they pulled him closer.

A slim thigh wrapped around his hip, and Zephyr arched into him. They broke apart for air, and the smile that lit Zephyr's face made Gawain grin in return. "That was kissing," Gawain said, and Zephyr nodded.

"I like kissing," Zephyr lifted his head, and Gawain obliged him with another, just as deep, tongues meeting and twining.

Gawain slid his hands down along the scaled, naked sides of his little dragon, the skin and scales blending perfectly, the only difference in the temperature of the scales compared to human skin. They were far more flexible and somewhat of a raised imprint, like a thick scarring, than the rough and thick scales Zephyr bore in his true form. Gawain followed the lines down until he curved a hand over one perky ass cheek and squeezed. Zephyr purred deep in his chest and writhed.

"More," Zephyr gasped out.

Gawain moved down his body, kissing and nipping as he went, and spread Zephyr's thighs with his shoulders. A thick cock with a pearly drop of precum at the trip throbbed along a trim abdomen, balls high and tight, the little dragon close. He smelled of fire and a hint of blood, the sharp tang of copper in the air during a fight, adrenaline pumping through veins. Gawain looked up, checking, and Zephyr was up on his elbows, biting his bottom lip, watching eagerly. Gawain smiled at him before lowering his mouth and sucking on the plump cock head. Zephyr jolted, gasping, and a hand grabbed his hair while hips lifted from the bed and pushed his cock deeper into Gawain's mouth.

No shy blushing virgin here, and Zephyr's eager fearlessness inspired Gawain to suck harder while his fingers explored the cleft of Zephyr's ass. He found his target when Zephyr snarled sharply, and all but slammed his hips down on his fingers, seeking more. Fangs bared, Zephyr was wild in his arousal, squirming while Gawain sucked on his cock and fucked him with a single digit, careful not to hurt him. Gawain pulled away, gasping, and reminded himself he had to be cautious, even with Zephyr being so enthusiastic. Zephyr whined in distress when he pulled away.

"No, more, my Gawain. Please," Zephyr whimpered, hands reaching for him.

"Need oil from my sidebag," Gawain soothed.

"Why?" So confused and needy, Zephyr twisted on the bed and sat up fast, grabbing Gawain before he could slip from the bed and head for his sidebags on the table.

Tossing aside any awkwardness he might have felt with anyone else, Gawain answered. "If you want me to play with your ass more, I need oil to ease the way, or I can hurt you. Human males don't get wet when aroused back there, so oil is important."

Lust cleared enough from Zephyr's eyes that the dragon's curiosity and surprise shone brightly in the ember depths. "Why wouldn't they? Evern and Axton mated while we were camped. Human bodies don't ready themselves for mating?"

Gawain leaned his head back and breathed past the laugh bubbling in his chest. He smiled down at Zephyr. "Humans aren't as efficient as other species when it comes to mating. Our failing. But one rectified by oils and the like."

Zephyr grinned at him; fangs bright in the candlelight. "I am not human. My Gawain will mount me, and we'll be happy together."

Zephyr tugged, and Gawain found himself on his back, cotton sheets cool on his skin, and Zephyr crawled on top of him. Leaning down, his little dragon straddled Gawain's hips, hands running over the ridges of the muscles along his belly and hips. "Mate with me." Zephyr asked softly, leaning forward and brushing their lips together.

"I don't want to hurt you," Gawain protested, tossing his head back into the pillows when a hand wrapped around his cock and stroked firmly.

"You won't," came the whisper from the shadows as Zephyr sat back.

Gawain groaned, and his hands wrapped around slim hips when the head of his cock kissed the tight muscle of Zephyr's hole. He was about to pull away, afraid to hurt his dragon by going in dry, when a gentle tingle of magic swept across Zephyr and showered down over Gawain. Prickling his skin, the magic danced in the space between them before dissipating, then Zephyr pushed down, and Gawain was inside his dragon a couple of inches. Tight, incredibly tight, soft hot flesh welcomed him inside. Zephyr cried out, and Gawain was afraid he'd hurt his young lover, but then Zephyr rocked himself downward, one hand on Gawain's chest to hold himself up, the other guiding Gawain deep into his heat, not stopping until his buttocks rested on Gawain and he could go no deeper.

"How..." Gawain gave up asking as Zephyr rolled his hips, and he thrust up instinctively.

"Mate with me, my Gawain," Zephyr begged, fingers gripping his pecs and fangs catching the light. "More!"

Gawain gave up resisting and took over, driving himself up as hard as he could while pulling Zephyr down on his cock. Zephyr's cries were desperate and called to something dark inside of Gawain, something that wanted to pin his lover to the bed and ride him until they were both reduced to ashes.

Gawain shouted when muscles gripped his cock tighter than anything he'd ever felt, and he flipped them in the bed, wrapping his arms around Zephyr and thrusting deep and fast. Zephyr spurred him on, legs around his hips, heels digging into his buttocks, hands frantically touching and gripping every part he could reach.

Human shaped he may be, but every cry and growl that poured from his sweetly human lips was all dragon, and he fucked back up into Gawain as he thrust down, his heated core milking every groan and sharp breath from Gawain. He was bowled over by pleasure, Zephyr matching him in desperation as sweat dripped from Gawain onto his gorgeous body. Gawain grunted with each thrust, Zephyr's hips rocking with each one, chasing him as he withdrew and making them meet with a clash on each downward stroke.

Trapped in lust and arousal, Gawain almost didn't see the glow of the scales that lined Zephyr's form. As embers flared to life when a banked fire was stoked and air fueled the slumbering coals, Zephyr's scales lit from within, fiery and hot. Zephyr arched into him, ass clamping on his cock, and Gawain swallowed the cry pushed from Zephyr as he came, kissing his dragon. Wet, almost painfully hot seed shot from Zephyr's cock, and Zephyr came apart in his arms, shuddering.

Gawain came on the tail end of Zephyr's climax, his orgasm erupting. He lost all his senses as his release crashed through his nerves and burned the air from his lungs. Pulsing deep inside his dragon, Gawain collapsed, pressing Zephyr down into the bedding.

Fingers trailing over his shoulders and a steady, satisfied purr gradually brought him out of his post-coital haze. With some effort, he lifted his head and smiled down at the very smug dragon beaming back up at him. "Are you well?" He had to ask. They'd exploded there at the end, and Gawain had never been that desperate or frenzied before. Zephyr's human form was so much smaller than Gawain, and despite the strength in his lissome extremities, Gawain worried. His scales were no longer glowing, the lines quiescent and blending with the shadows.

Zephyr smiled and kissed along Gawain's jaw, gentle nips on his chin that tickled and warmed. "My Gawain is a wonderful mate." A quick lick to his lips and arms wrapped around his neck as Zephyr lifted into a kiss.

Gawain was still buried deep inside Zephyr's sweet heat, and as the kiss deepened, his body roused. Zephyr tightened his legs around his waist and slipped his tongue into Gawain's mouth to angle with Gawain's. He thrust his hips, unable to resist, and Zephyr welcomed him deeper.

12

Dressed in a robe borrowed from the mage, Zephyr sat on the back of Gawain's warhorse, the beast's ears turning back and forth as the retinue prepared to depart the market square. There were booths along the edge of the square, and a bakery was open across the way, many people bustling in and out. It smelled wonderful, and Zephyr wanted to get down and go investigate, but Gawain was very firm that Zephyr stay on the horse. Zephyr had one hand in the braided mane of the beast and left the reins alone, not knowing the first thing about guiding a horse—not that he thought the warhorse would listen. It was growing accustomed to his presence on its back, but it still had an awareness of him that was due to his predatory nature. The horse knew he was a dragon, even if he still wore his human form. Gawain spoke to Tristan a few paces away, the two men discussing the state of their wounded people. Zephyr had no desire to end up back in the uncomfortable wagon, so he stayed quiet. No sense drawing attention to himself.

The robe covered him from head to toes, and he refused to wear socks or boots, the articles of clothing irritating and making him feel as if he would trip with every step. The robe was lightweight and had a cowl he could pull up, which even now obscured his features and hid the oddness of his hair and the scales that patterned his skin. The innkeeper had gotten a close look at him as they came down the stairs into the common room for breakfast, his startled reaction prompting Tristan to unpack a robe and urge Zephyr to change.

He was glad he wasn't in his natural form. The strangers on the road and in town would not take kindly to a dragon walking into town, even if accompanied by knights. He was a thinking, feeling being who was capable of intelligent speech and communication and yet he would be greeted with fear and violence. Gawain was taking him to the palace, the place where he grew up, and the Queen, the dominant female who ruled this kingdom, wanted to meet him, but he wondered if she would react badly, like the humans back in Morvain.

Where would he go then? Surrounded by humans, all with the potential to become violent, what would come of him if the Queen turned him away? His gaze fell on Gawain, his knight as handsome as ever. Long black hair tied back in a thick braid that fell past his shoulders, beard trimmed that morning, his armor gleaming, Gawain was a jewel amongst the dull colors of the humans around him.

Possessiveness and a desire to protect, to transform and clutch Gawain in his claws and disappear into the clouds high above and fly away to some place that no one would ever threaten them again welled up from deep inside. A night of kisses and mating merely cemented the claim Gawain had upon Zephyr's heart and soul. His knight was worth a few alarmed glances and potential violence. And if the Queen refused to relinquish her nestmate? Zephyr would fight for mating rights.

The horse shifted beneath him, restless. He pulled himself from his musings and sniffed the air. The wind changed and took away the lovely scents from the bakery. Humans, horses, other furry beats he had no names for, and a variety of unpleasant odors assaulted his senses, but there was a particular one that caught his attention. Humans milled about in the square where the inn resided, a main thorough-fare for the population. Wagons, pulled by shorter versions of the warhorses that carried the knights, and a shepherd guiding a small flock went by, and two men draped in cloaks followed behind the sheep.

A spark of ozone, similar to that of lightning building in the clouds before a strike, stirred the air. Magic. Zephyr called on his aurasight and the auras of every living being around him burst into view.

The men in cloaks were mages, though not as strong as the nameless one who haunted Zephyr's dreams. These men were attempting to conceal themselves from everyone around them, dark brown cloaks and cowls hiding their features. They passed by Zephyr where he sat on the big warhorse and approached Gawain and Tristan from behind, peeling away from the flock of sheep.

Tristan reacted first, but not in time—the mage stopped speaking and looked around suspiciously, but he was searching in the wrong direction. Gawain put a hand on his sword, but the men were too close.

Zephyr gathered his own magic, instinct and fear guiding his actions, and he screamed, one hand lifting, fingers pointed toward the mages who were lifting their own hands, fingers twisting spells before casting. Fire and light spun through the air, horses neighing in panic, humans shouting and ducking out of the way. Tristan saw the magic hurtling toward them and grabbed Gawain, throwing them off to the side and to the ground.

Dragonfire caught the mages just as they released their spells, which impacted on the cobblestones where Tristan and

Gawain had been standing. The stone blackened and split, the spells discharging in a burst of sparks. Dragonfire enveloped their cloaks, and they screamed, batting at their clothing. Zephyr jumped from the horse and darted forward, his human body glimmering in fire that danced over his arms and shoulders, the scales on his hands glowing bright, white-hot and brilliant, and he released the magic. It knocked into the two men and sent them rolling across the square. They came to a stop when they smacked into the base of the fountain in the center of the square, clothing smoldering. They didn't move.

Smoke and ozone swirled in the morning breeze. An unnatural stillness settled, a shocked silence within those present. The knights moved first—Axton and Evern helped Gawain and Tristan to their feet while Bedivere and Avril dashed across the square toward the two mages.

Zephyr forgot about his prey and dashed to Gawain, running his hands over every inch he could reach, searching for injuries. "My Gawain! Are you well? They were going to hurt you!"

Gawain pulled Zephyr into his arms. "My little dragon." Gawain hugged him and lifted him into the air, squeezing him until Zephyr squeaked. Gawain gentled his hold and lowered him back to his feet. Gawain cupped his face and gazed down at him in wonder. "You saved us. Thank you, Zephyr."

"Not hurt?" Zephyr asked, worried. He looked unharmed, but he had to be sure.

"Not hurt. You?"

"I stopped them," Zephyr said. He was fine. His magic was depleted again, but not as badly as it would have been if he had transformed then tried to stop the mages. He would have been too late.

Gawain gathered him close and turned to his knights, who were dragging the mages back. "Are they alive?"

"Aye," Avril tossed one at Gawain's feet, and put her sword to his throat. The man was burnt badly along the back and side of his face, but he was conscious. He stared up at Zephyr in terror, mouth working. The other human was still limp, clearly knocked out. Sword point to his throat, the conscious man held still.

"Who are you and why did you attack us?" Gawain asked, voice cold and unforgiving. The man finally tore his gaze away from Zephyr and stammered as he answered Gawain.

"Hershel, sir," the man gasped, sweat beading on his brow. "A man from Medilan hired us. Said we would be rewarded if we managed to kill you and the mage," Hershel gasped, pointing with a shaky hand to Tristan who glowered down at him. "Said he needed you out of the way. You've got something he wants."

"Did he tell you what that was?"

The man gasped, coughing. "No. Paid me and Gus here to kill you both and as many of the knights you've got with you as we could. Said he'd get what he was after himself once you were dead."

Gawain spoke to Tristan, dread building in Zephyr as he came to the same realization. "He's here."

Tristan nodded, and set his gaze out over the square, looking carefully. Magic stirred, and Zephyr felt the mage investigating out further than he could see, trying to find the one who wanted them dead.

"Did he tell you a name?" Gawain demanded. "Do you know who he is?"

The mage shook his head and grimaced in pain. "No, sir. I knew he was a mage, and powerful too. He blurred his features with a spell, but his accent was Melidane for certain. I'd know it anywhere."

Zephyr went cold and buried his face in Gawain's shoulder.

The mage who haunted his nightmares was there, nearby, somewhere.

The man Gawain called a magistrate took the enemy mages away, shackled in bespelled iron, their magic useless. Gawain explained he was something called a High Justiciar, which gave him the authority to pass judgment, and the attempted murder of a royal was punishable by death. He chose instead life imprisonment, the two men able to identify the mage who hired them by the man's voice, and Gawain wanted them still breathing in case they needed to testify. Zephyr wasn't too clear on what it all meant, but he understood enough that the men might be of help and his knight was showing mercy. If it were up to Zephyr, he would have charred them down to melted fat and eaten them.

Zephyr sniffed in disdain when the talkative one kept staring at him with a mix of awe and terror, though he appreciated the terror more than he would admit aloud. Gawain might not approve.

"Stay here or make our way to the capital?" Tristan asked Gawain. His knight frowned, thinking. They were still in the square, but everyone was armed, the knights arrayed around then in a half-circle, facing outward. Tristan had given them all small charms that hung from their chainmail shirts that would glow if there was magic nearby that was inimical. He stressed that it wasn't perfect, but it would serve as a warning for those knights who didn't have magic of their own.

Zephyr was under Gawain's arm, the knight refusing to let him go, not that he wanted to go anywhere. Gawain responded to Tristan, both men tense. "If we stay here, we risk townspeople getting hurt. If we leave and ride hard for the capital, we risk another ambush on the road."

"Bad decision either way."

Gawain nodded. "See how many men can be spared from the town watch, and if there are enough mounts. We're safe inside the castle confines; the wards should keep the mage hunting us out."

Zephyr perked up at that. Spells that could keep out the evil mage sounded wonderful. He tugged on Gawain's tunic. Gawain looked down at him, giving him a soft squeeze around his shoulders with his arm. "My Gawain, if your territory can keep him out, we should go there."

Gawain sighed then gave a slow nod. "This is a bad choice, no matter how we look at it. There's no wards here in the town, and I don't want to risk any innocents. This place doesn't have anywhere secure enough for us to bunk down and wait for reinforcements." Gawain spoke to his cousin. "We leave in an hour."

Zephyr was not enjoying the pace they traveled at. The wagons had been nearly emptied, and most of the gear was left behind in the small town they'd left. The horses who were pulling the wagons were outfitted with saddles purchased in the town, and a dozen town watch guards rode with them. Jon had remained behind with Felix, the blacksmith, and the few servants in the retinue, holed up at the town healer's residence. Both Jon and Felix had objected, but they quieted when Gawain told them he would send knights for them once they got back to the capital.

Gawain doubted the mage would bother with them and would instead chase after Gawain and Tristan and the wagons, likely thinking that there might be a dragon hiding in one of the wagons. The one that had held the blacksmith's portable forge could probably fit a malnourished dragon inside, and so they tacked down the coverings and brought it along, even though it was nearly empty.

Zephyr held tight to Gawain, the whole retinue moving along the wider, smoother roads at a fast clip. Sora traveled a short distance ahead of them, calling for travelers on the road to move aside. Most heard the thunder of many hooves echoing along the roadway and looked over their shoulders before frantically spurring their own mounts or conveyances to the side of the road. Those that saw them coming moved aside well in advance, so they were making good time, or so Gawain assured him every couple of hours.

Tristan stayed with the larger wagon, giving credence to the ruse that Zephyr was in the wagon, even going so far as to put a showy spell upon it that looked like a shield but would illuminate the direction an attacking spell came from if it was hit. Zephyr liked that idea—it was something a dragon would do.

They stopped a hour or so after sunset, the roads thinned out of travelers, but there were still enough people to gawk at them as they went by. Spare mounts were switched out, legs were stretched, food and water consumed, then they were back on the road. Gawain's spare mount was just as huge as the first one and seemingly tireless. Zephyr felt magic echo across the group a few hours later, well past the midnight mark, and he feared it was their enemy, but the magic swelled in a rush of energy and collected on the horses, knights, and the watchmen. Horses snorted, and men sat up straighter in the saddles, Tristan's magic giving them energy to keep going as the tiny suns he sent racing ahead of them lit the way.

Zephyr woke from an uneasy sleep, blinking at the sunlight poking at his eyes. Dawn was breaking over the horizon, and Zephyr though at first he was seeing mountains in the distance, but then he squinted, and the shapes in the distance solidified into straight vertical lines and towering edifices.

"The capital," Gawain murmured in his ear. "And the castle in the heart of the city. We've made good time. We'll be there in a couple of hours."

Zephyr woke fully at those words and watched as the city, and the looming towers of the castle grew closer. The road was packed with humans, wagons, riders, and people walking along. Their pace slowed the closer they got, but there was an increase in mounted knights in the crowd. Their numbers grew as knights hailed their prince and cut their mounts through the crowd, joining their ranks and surrounding the members of the original retinue in a wall of armor and horseflesh.

Details of the buildings came into stark relief and the number of people around them grew exponentially, and Zephyr grew more anxious the closer they got. He turned his face and buried his nose in Gawain's shoulder, and his knight pulled his cloak tighter around him, hiding him from any curious glances. It also kept Zephyr from seeing what was around him, but that was perfectly fine with him—he was raised in near solitude, and so many humans and animals and the accompanying noise was overwhelming.

Gawain worried about Zephyr, his dragon shivering against his shoulder. He held as tightly to him as he could and without hurting him, and he wanted nothing more than to get Zephyr into the safe confines of the castle grounds.

Shouts up ahead on High Street had him squinting against the midday sun. Pikes and banners of the castle guards cleared the road, and a mounted guardsman cut through the ranks of the squadron clearing the avenue. "Your Highness!" Captain Nerys called, her bright blonde hair catching the sunlight along with her polished breastplate etched with the symbol of the Royal Guards.

"Captain!" Gawain hailed in return.

Captain Nerys wove her roan gelding through the knights, and came alongside him. "Your Highness, I've cleared the avenue ahead all the way to the castle gate. Her Majesty is most anxious to see you." Nerys eyed Zephyr curiously, one brow arched high, but she said nothing.

"Can't keep my sister waiting," Gawain said with a grin.

The avenue was indeed cleared, the castle guard making a clear path up the slight hill along the opulent grand homes of the nobles and wealthy that clustered closest to the castle grounds. They were half-timbered with the upper levels made from thick logs, the siding painted bright white, and the lower levels made from quarried stone blocks. Iron lanterns swung in the slight breeze, and the marble door frames were carved with sigils and fantastic animals. The streets were clean and flowers and blooming bushes decorated stoops and windowsills framed by shutters painted in bright colors. Flags and heraldic banners hung over the doors of each home, signifying which families lived within.

"I would strongly suggest we hurry," Captain Nerys agreed.

Playful though their exchange was, Gawain heard the urgency. It matched his own—Zephyr would only be safe inside the castle. The wards around the castle were as old as the building itself, set deep in the earth, impossible to bypass, and they prevented any magic that wasn't keyed to them from passing. Gawain was of royal blood, and all he needed to do was consciously invite or carry something or someone new across the ward line and their presence would be allowed unless revoked at a later time.

Gawain urged his stallion to increase his pace, and the big horse tossed his head and answered with a burst of speed, the ringing of hooves on the pavers that made up this older and far wealthier portion of the city echoing loudly off the stone facades of the old houses that lined the avenue.

The castle gate rose above the end of High Street, a dozen mounted knights able to pass abreast through the gateway, the great iron and oak drawbridge already lowered in welcome, the huge chains that could lift it shut bigger around than a grown man. Gawain gripped Zephyr with both arms, his stallion carrying them over the wards that lined the inner edge of the moat, and the magic shimmered along his skin, startling Zephyr.

"Easy, easy. Just the wards around the castle. You're safe now," Gawain whispered to his dragon, then they were inside the castle walls.

The courtyard was huge, lined with white and gray stones bigger than a warhorse, and the great doors of the castle itself were open in welcome at the top of a dozen steps.

Gawain saw his sister, dressed in royal blue, standing apart from her ladies in waiting and the guards. She wore a simple gold coronet around her brow, as she was outside her private quarters. Elise smiled wide when she saw him, relief in her eyes.

She came down a few steps as he drew his horse to a halt, the knights and guards behind him drawing to a halt as well, servants and stable hands entering the teeming mass of horses to assist the knights.

Her smile in welcome turned to an expression of concern when she saw Zephyr, but he wasn't going to explain out in the open where everyone could hear.

Legs complaining, Gawain dismounted, sliding from the saddle with Zephyr in his arms. He strode for his sister, who gathered her long skirts in her hands. "Gawain—," she started, but he kept going, cradling Zephyr to his chest, his dragon shivering and thankfully still completely covered.

"Sorry for the rush, Your Majesty, but my friend here is very tired and needs to rest." Gawain loaded his words with meaning, and Elise caught on quickly, following alongside him as he entered the castle and headed for his quarters.

The castle was full of servants, who bowed as they passed, and Gawain regretted not being able to acknowledge them but for a nod as he swept on by.

"Gawain, why are we all but running? And who is this? Where's the dragon?" Elise hissed under her breath, smiling brilliantly and saying hello as they passed another servant.

"I'll explain behind closed doors, Sister. He's a friend."

"You better! This is most undignified. We're nearly running!"

"Like you haven't run through your own castle before," Gawain quipped as he climbed the stairs, Elise keeping up with him. She huffed out a breath in annoyance but didn't deny it.

His quarters were not far from his sister's, on the same floor and at the opposite end of the long hall. He was never more thankful that his sister insisted he remain in the castle after he was knighted instead of moving to the barracks with the rest of his ennobled peers, as there was no privacy there, and the balcony attached to his bedroom overlooked the inner courtyard and the private gardens of the queen.

Gawain paused long enough for Elise to open the door to his chambers, and Gawain carried Zephyr inside. She shut the door then spun around with hands on her hips and a glare. "Why on earth did we all but sprint up here without a proper greeting, and where in the world is the dragon that Tristan's message said you rescued? And who is this?"

Gawain set Zephyr down on a low couch in his sitting room, and he brushed back the hood. Zephyr smiled at him, and the worry he was carrying since they entered the city dissipated. "There you are," Gawain murmured and pressed a gentle kiss to Zephyr's forehead. "Feeling better?"

"I am." Zephyr peeked over his shoulder, ember eyes wide. "Is she your nestmate?" Gawain sat beside Zephyr and helped him shrug off the cloak, his beautiful hair tumbling about.

Elise stared, wide-eyed, mouth falling open a bit in surprise. Light came in from the high windows and danced over Zephyr, highlighting the scales on one side of his face, and the red strands in his hair. Zephyr smiled wide, fangs visible, and he gave a small wave. "Hello."

13

The human female looked very much like his knight, though she was shorter and not as muscular. Magic hovered around her of a similar feel to the tiny spark Gawain carried, though with more resemblance to Tristan's in power. Her hair was a far lighter color, more like the mage's, and just as long as her brother's, though she wore it loose, held back only by a circle of gold metal on her brow.

"Hello."

She blinked at him, coming out of her shock, and her eyes cataloged the small things that proved he was not truly human. She came closer and sat gingerly upon a small cushioned thing with squat wooden legs not far from where they sat on the odd bed thing with arms.

"Elise, this is Zephyr. He is..." Gawain began, but Zephyr gently interrupted him.

"I am Zephyr. Dragon. You are Gawain's nestmate."

"Nestmate." She stated, questioning. She tilted her head then made the mental leap. "Oh! We are siblings, yes. I am older by a handful of years. Gawain is my brother."

"Gawain is my knight." Zephyr had to make sure this

dominant female knew he was claiming Gawain and for more than fleeting and meaningless mating displays from young dragons learning how to enjoy pleasures.

"Your knight...?" She looked to her nestmate. Gawain flushed and took one of Zephyr's hands in his, gripping firmly.

"He has grown very attached to me—we have grown very attached to each other—since we rescued him in Morvain." Gawain seemed to be telling his nestmate something, extra meaning in his words, and the female named Elise was confused for a long moment before her eyes fell to their joined hands.

"Attached! Oh, I see. How unexpected."

"Gawain is mine now," Zephyr declared. She must understand. Gawain was his, and he was not giving him up.

Her lips twitched then finally broke into a smile, eyes glimmering with humor. "Gawain, I do believe you've just been acquired by a dragon."

"He's been calling me his since the rescue." Gawain shrugged, not bothered. "I don't understand exactly, but our relationship has changed a bit since Zephyr took human form a few nights ago."

Zephyr frowned, not liking that Gawain was not sure. He turned to his knight and leaned into him. Gawain smiled down at him, affection in his eyes. "Gawain is mine. My mate."

"Your mate...?" Gawain's eyes went wide as the words sank in.

"Oh dear," Elise murmured, and she gathered up her skirts and stood. "Little brother, I'll be seeing you and our guest later. I think you both need to talk things out. I'll go see Tristan and sort out everything else." She left the room, firmly shutting the door behind her.

Gawain spoke as soon as his nestmate was gone. "Mate?"

He took both of Zephyr's hands and tugged gently until Zephyr was in his lap. Big hands gripped his waist, and Zephyr rested on Gawain's muscular chest, face to face with his knight. Gawain gave him a soft kiss on his lips then pulled back enough to see each other as he spoke. "Explain what you mean by mate. I don't think you mean the act of sex or pleasure. Or not just that."

Zephyr squirmed, confused. "My Gawain?" A question. Gawain was his, wasn't he? Gawain had taken him to his nest, cared for him, brought him food, and slept beside him since Gawain chased away the bad humans. "Gawain cared for me like a dragon who wants to keep another. Does Gawain not want me in his hoard? I want Gawain in my hoard, but I don't have one. I only have Gawain."

"I'm human, little dragon. Humans do not have hoards, not like dragons do. My sister has a hoard, but that's the royal treasury."

Zephyr's heart sank, feeling like it was in freefall after hitting a storm and its wings could no longer work. He knew he'd have some explaining to do once they got to Gawain's den, but the divide between their species suddenly seemed vast. He tried anyway. "My Gawain—," he stopped and exhaled hard before sucking in a deep breath and trying to be as clear as he could. "You save me, take me back to your nest, help heal me, protect me, sleep beside me, then I display desire for pleasures and Gawain teaches me how humans mate. You bring me to your stone den, and I tell nestmate Gawain is mine. Is Gawain not my mate? Is Gawain not mine? Gawain is my hoard, I have only Gawain."

Gawain's face was a mix of confusion, surprise, and something else he couldn't identify. Zephyr's heart cracked, and he slipped from Gawain's lap and evaded his hands, stepping away and wiping at his face. His cheeks were wet, liquid falling from his eyes. He wiped them again, confused and frustrated and hurt, and he felt like a fool. He was a dragon that forgot he wasn't human.

The sadness in Zephyr's gaze almost broke him. Gawain stood, following after Zephyr, terrified his dragon would leave and he'd never see him again. It was irrational, but his racing heart and spiking adrenaline wouldn't let him take the chance.

Zephyr cried, wiping at his face, and Gawain went to him. Zephyr tried to spin away, sniffling, but Gawain hugged him to his chest, pressing kisses to red and black curls. He was tense for a short moment, then his slim arms came up around him and clung. His dragon cried, muffled sobs shaking his small human body. "Shh, little dragon, shhh. I'm sorry I didn't understand. I didn't ask for you to explain from the very beginning, and I am sorry that I let it go this long. You are mine, Zephyr. Mine, just as I am yours. I already decided days ago that belonging to you was something that I wanted."

He whispered it over and over, rocking Zephyr gently, hoping he would hear and believe. "I am yours. You are mine."

Zephyr sniffled, wiping his face on his tunic. Watery and reddened eyes peeked up at him, and Gawain gave him a soft kiss on the tip of his pert nose. Zephyr blinked at him, confused, but something like hope building in the ember depths of his eyes. "Gawain—you—want me?"

"Yes, I do. I love you." Saying it aloud was easier than anything he'd ever done, and as he gave voice to the words he knew they'd been true since he saw Zephyr crouched in a cave, terrified and afraid to trust. "I love you with everything that I am."

Zephyr pulled back a bit and wiped at his face then frowned at his fingers. He glanced back up, a lock of hair falling over his face, and Gawain brushed it back. "Gawain loves this human body. Does Gawain not love true form? I am dragon."

Gawain took a moment to gather his thoughts, refusing to let any chance of misunderstanding hurt Zephyr again. "I love you. I love your true form, you as the beautiful and fantastic dragon who loves to snuggle and scent mark me. Sleeping beside you, talking to you, just existing next to you is amazing and something I never want to give up. You are so brave and loving, even after what's been done to you, and I never want you to be someone or something you are not." Gawain took Zephyr's hand in his and kissed his slim fingers, the scales glinting in the light. "I can't make love to you as a dragon, I don't think our parts match, so if you want sex and pleasures, being in this form on occasion might be necessary, but I will never prefer this form over your true one. So, if you want to be a dragon forever and never again take this form, I will still love you, and I'll learn what I must to make you a happy and content dragon."

Zephyr stared in surprise, and his heart sang, the headiness of Gawain's words as close to the thrill of a mating flight as he would ever get. Gawain's aura reinforced the truth of his words, and Zephyr marveled at the human man who meant every word he spoke.

"My Gawain?" he whispered.

"My Zephyr," Gawain answered, a possessive rumble under the words.

Zephyr stood on tiptoe and kissed Gawain, whimpering and needing the reassurance of his touch, his taste and scent.

He jumped up, and Gawain caught him, all without breaking the kiss, and he wrapped his arms and legs around his knight. Chainmail and leather dug at his skin, but he needed Gawain too much to care.

Mouths sealed together, tongues twining, Gawain walked a few steps until they tumbled onto a weird thing with a thick soft surface and many blankets. Gawain fell to the side, thankfully not crushing him as he still wore his metal shirt and armor.

It was a fancy bed, more so than the one at the inn. A few pillows but not many, and it was in a frame with four corners and a canopy overhead. It was encased in carved wood along the head, its pillars carved as well and painted in bright colors, figures and fruits and animals dancing along the wood.

Zephyr crawled onto it and went to his hands and knees, before lowering his shoulders to the bed and spreading his knees, getting as close as he could to a dragon's enticement to mate, presenting for a more dominant dragon. He looked back over his shoulder, and Gawain stared at his rump, breathing hard. "My Gawain. I want."

Gawain undressed as fast as he could, only taking care with his weapons, setting them beside the bed gently, then stripping himself of the rest of his armor and clothing.

Gawain climbed onto the bed, mounting Zephyr with open mouthed kisses and gentle nips along his back and shoulders. Gawain kissed the side of his neck, and Zephyr arched up into him, desperate for his mate.

"Please," he whimpered, and Gawain groaned, settling his weight on Zephyr. Fingers slid between his ass cheeks and touched that sensitive part of him, and Zephyr spared just enough thought to stir magic, letting the fingers playing around the outside to slip inside with ease, a delightful burn and stretch. He cried out, shivering in need, then the fingers were gone, and his mate's thick cock slid in a few inches.

Zephyr growled, fingers tearing at the blankets, and pushed up into the thrust, seating his mate deep inside. Gawain let out a long, low moan of primal satisfaction, breath hot over the back of Zephyr's neck, strong hands holding him in place. The first thrust was deep and lit up a spot inside that made him scream in joy and lust, and he arched himself as best he could, demanding more. Gawain gave it to him, hips slapping against his ass, and Zephyr purred loudly, encouraging his mate, needing more. Gawain answered, hands sliding along his body as his cock worked deep inside Zephyr, so big and stretching to the point of pain. His mate rode him hard, and Zephyr shared his pleasure with every gasp and scream torn from his throat.

Gawain mounted him fully, as any dragon would his mate,

fucking hard and thoroughly, making Zephyr take his full length and pushing even deeper before pulling out, the blunt head stretching his hole wide before pushing back in without hesitation, each stroke smooth and commanding. Zephyr worked his hips, chasing the pleasure, refusing to lay passively even as his mate dominated him. He wanted Gawain to feel everything, and he flexed around the hot length buried to the hilt inside. Gawain groaned, and a hand grasped Zephyr's cock and stroked it in time with the thrusts deep into his core.

He came, seed shooting from his cock, and he screamed, the sound echoing off the walls, then Gawain thrust hard enough to push him flat to the bed, cock pulsing deep inside, hot and wet and everything he needed. Gawain breathed hard in his ear, sweaty and heavy, and kissed Zephyr's shoulder then his cheek, hips rocking as they came down together from their climaxes.

Exhaustion and release came for him, and his eyes drifted shut in slumber, but not before he heard Gawain's whisper. "My dragon, my love."

❧ 14 ❧

Gawain woke slowly, the afternoon sun in his eyes. It took him a moment to realize he was home, in his bedchamber, and he was warm and comfortable. His cheek rested on a scaled shoulder, and the dragon breathing softly beneath him took up all the room on the bed, his long tail trailing off the side and to the floor. A wing was curved over the top of him, keeping him warm since they were still on top of the blankets, never making it under them before passing out.

He stretched, muscles aching from days in the saddle then a swift, hard, powerfully satisfying fuck that left no doubt that he wanted his dragon forever.

He sat up carefully, not wanting to hurt the delicate membrane of Zephyr's wing. A gentle nudge and the wing pulled back, and Zephyr stretched. Wings went high until they hit the canopy with a thunk, and Zephyr blinked himself awake and looked around in a daze. The remains of the tunic were under his fronts legs, shredded when Zephyr regained his natural form.

Zephyr eyed him cautiously, ducking his muzzle shyly, one long claw scratching idly at the covers. Gawain reached out and put a hand under his chin, the scales rougher now, thicker and hard to the touch. Zephyr was far stronger in this form, and he let Gawain lift his head so they could meet eye to eye.

"I love you, my dragon," Gawain said clearly, sincere. "I love you in this form, and any other. Dragon or man, I love you."

Zephyr's ember eyes glowed, and happiness suffused every line of his beautiful form. He glowed, a subtle glimmer of fire and magic, the lines of his scales flashing before subsiding. "I love my knight." Zephyr's voice was once again the deeper rumble he'd first heard, faint hissing underlying each word. "I love Gawain."

Gawain hugged Zephyr around his neck, and Zephyr rested his great head on his back, fronts legs and wings hugging him in return. Zephyr was so warm, his muscular form graceful and deadly, but he moved with such care. He rested in Zephyr's embrace, relaxing, content to remain like that forever.

Zephyr struggled to contain his happiness, afraid he would break Gawain's bed and his den if he jumped around and did a dance to celebrate their mating. Gawain smelled of happiness too, along with sweat, musky seed, and arousal from their mating earlier. He relished how Gawain felt against him, smooth and warm human skin against his scales. He sniffed, addicted to his mate's scent, and licked along his shoulder, churring happily.

Gawain laughed, pulling back a bit, smiling at him, blue eyes bright with joy. "That tickled."

Zephyr snuck in another lick, along his thigh, and his mate laughed, twitching, hands on his nose. "That tickles! Stop it!" Zephyr preened, pleased to make his mate laugh. He would lick Gawain later when he wasn't expecting it. His laugh was wonderful.

Gawain stretched, and Zephyr eyed the muscles and skin that rippled as his mate groaned then slid from bed. He looked tired. "Come back to bed. Nest is warm, if small. Sleep more."

"I would love to, my dragon, but I need to speak to my sister. I'm sure Tristan has told her everything that's happened since we got you out of Morvain, but I need to tell her I'm getting married." Gawain walked toward a door off the side of the bedroom, and Zephyr slid carefully from the odd bed when his mate gestured for him to follow.

"What is married?" Zephyr asked, ducking and pulling his wings in as they entered a room lined in white stone that smelled of metal, magic, and water. A large basin in the floor to one side soon filled with water, that came from metal sticks stuck at one end. Magic hummed in the depths of the room, and Zephyr eased into his own magic, seeing the bespelled workings under the stone that pulled the water to the room through long metal pipes. The water came out hot, and he realized it was a bath, the tub a permanent structure instead of being picked up and moved from place to place.

Gawain slipped into the water and dunked himself, reaching for soap in a tiny tray next to the tub.

"Marriage is the human equivalent of mating," Gawain explained, scrubbing himself. "I think, at least. Marriage for royals it is a lifelong bond, only broken by death or treason, or something like barrenness if heirs are required."

"When dragons find the ones they want forever, they mate for life," Zephyr offered, settling down beside the bath, sniffing at the water as Gawain cleaned himself. "I will dance for you and display my wings and offer to share my hoard. We shall nest together and maybe have egglings."

Gawain paused in his scrubbing. "I can't lay any eggs. Can you?"

He wasn't a broodmother, but he knew some males had eggs. He would need to think about it. He was an eggling himself when they were taken, and such details weren't important to discuss in chains. "I don't think so. Wasn't taught such things. Eggs came when dragons wanted them."

Gawain went back to scrubbing, rinsing himself then climbing from the tub, letting the water drain out through a hole in the floor. Zephyr wondered where it went.

"We're not the same species so I don't think we need to worry about eggs. We can talk about kids whenever we think we're ready. No rush. I need to get dressed, then we can go talk to Elise."

"Yes," Zephyr purred. "Shall do marriage and mating with my Gawain."

Gawain rubbed a hand down Zephyr's neck in a fond gesture, and he churred happily.

Zephyr kept his wings in close so as not to hit the walls, following closely behind Gawain as they walked down a hallway toward an open set of doors. Evening sunlight poured across the floor and walls in a fiery orange, and they stepped out into a garden full of trees and flowers.

There was space for him to relax his wings, and Zephyr sniffed at flowers and bushes as he followed his knight deeper into the garden.

"Oh, my goodness." Elise gasped as she stood up from the bench in the center of the garden. She waved back some guards, the humans staring at Zephyr warily, but he didn't sense any violence from them. Tristan was in the garden too, and Zephyr waved a wingtip at him in greeting.

Gawain and Zephyr stopped, and Zephyr sat on his haunches, the wing closest to Gawain coming out a bit to curve along his back, claiming his mate in front of the female. She stared at him, her aura a pleasant mix of blues and greens and some gold. A strong female, very much in charge, but kind.

"Greetings, Zephyr." She dipped her chin, smiling. "I am Elise, Queen of Kentaine, and as you know already, I am Gawain's older sister." She paused, eyes taking in his form, and he was glad her aura showed no sign of fear. "Your magic is impressive, and I am so pleased to see you feel safe enough to reclaim your true form in my home. You are safe behind the wards of the castle. The mage hunting you cannot get past them, and I promise you he shall be stopped and brought to justice. Welcome, Zephyr, and I hope you choose to stay here in Kentaine."

"Thanksss," he replied, wondering what else to say. He churred at his mate, who put a hand on his shoulder, rubbing.

"Has Tristan briefed you?" Gawain asked.

"He has," Elise answered, and her expression was somewhat smug and teasing. "Though, I think some things have been left out. Do you have something to tell me, brother?"

"Gawain is my mate," Zephyr blurted out, a bit of smoke escaping his nostrils. He brought his tail forward and curled the end around one of Gawain's legs. "We share a nest."

Gawain coughed into his hand then stood as straight as he could while Zephyr hung off him. "I am informing you, My Queen, that I am marrying the dragon Zephyr and becoming his mate."

"Mate already," Zephyr made sure to clarify. "Gawain has mounted me and agreed to share life."

Gawain flushed, and Tristan laughed, shaking his head. Elise grew pink across her cheeks, but she smiled at Zephyr. "I will not ask for details, but since you've come to ask me formally, I must give an answer." She spoke to Zephyr. "As Gawain is technically my heir, he must ask for permission to marry, as any children he may have will also be my heirs." She clasped her hands together and eyed her brother, who stared back at his sister calmly. "It will push my governors into demanding I marry myself, but I was planning on it this year regardless. I give my blessing, little brother. You may marry your dragon."

Gawain turned and hugged Zephyr. He wrapped his

knight up in his front legs and wings, churring loudly, smoke rising around them.

Gawain almost stumbled when Zephyr crouched, bending one shoulder downward, and then lifted his wings, looking at Gawain expectedly.

He blinked in surprise. "Are you sure?"

"Mating flight. Gawain cannot fly, so fly with me. I am strong." Zephyr was sure.

Gawain hesitated for only a second then trusted his dragon.

Gawain sat carefully above Zephyr's wing joints and grabbed a neck spike. It was clipped short, but still long enough for him to grab it. Zephyr stood again, and it was not at all like riding a horse. Zephyr was coiled muscle and dangerous strength. Zephyr looked back at him. "Hold tight with legs. Don't let go."

"I'll never let go," Gawain promised. Tristan and Elise moved back, and then Zephyr crouched low, and with a jump and a snap of wings, they leapt into the air.

Together, they climbed higher into the sky, and Gawain shouted in amazement, Zephyr roaring with joy.

Zephyr and Gawain will return. There's an evil mage to defeat, and a wedding of the ages to plan. Thank you for reading, and I hope you've enjoyed the first part of their tale.

AFTERWORD

Thank you for reading Knight's Fire!

This has been a task undertaken with love and affection for my fans. The support from my readers keep the words coming and the series expanding.

Please consider leaving a review on Amazon and/or Goodreads. A review helps other readers decide to take a chance on a book, and helps indie authors like me. Happy reading!

Thank you,
    Sheena (SJ)

ALSO BY SJ HIMES

Scales of Honor

Knight's Fire

The Wolfkin Saga

Wolves of Black Pine

Wolf of the Northern Star

The Beacon Hill Sorcerer

The Necromancer's Dance

The Necromancer's Dilemma

The Necromancer's Reckoning

A History of Trouble (Collection)

Realms of Love

The Solstice Prince

Standalone

Saving Silas

Writing as Revella Hawthorne

Bred For Love: The Prince's Consort

Bred For Love: The King's Command

Bred For Love: A Royal Rebellion

ABOUT THE AUTHOR

My name is Sheena, and I have more pen names than I probably should. I write as SJ Himes, Revella Hawthorne, and Sheena Himes. I reside in the mountains of Maine (closer to Canada than I am to fresh lobster) on a 300 year-old farm beside a river in the woods. My companions are my furbabies: Micah, my large dog who hates birds; and Wolf and Silfur, two cats who love me but hate each other. I write romances with an emphasis on plot and character development, and almost all my characters are LGBTQ+ and that's on purpose. To keep current on what I'm working on and where to find me on social media, go to my website: www.sjhimes.com